The Gresham Chronicles

Books 1-3

SASKIA KNIGHT

DEDICATION

To my beautiful sister, Lynda. There can be no other sister so loving, so selfless, or so kind. Love you to the moon and back, sis. xx

CONTENTS

PROLOGUE

Norfolk, England 1206

Lady Angelique Gresham closed her eyes and fell back on the soft grass, relishing the heat of the summer sun on her eyelids and the sensuous tickle of wildflowers against her ankles. She sighed. "What a perfect day. If only it would last forever."

Lady Melisende Gresham gazed thoughtfully across the lush river valley to the castle, so solid and prosperous, and watched as the pennant flying atop the battlements snapped and fluttered briefly before changing direction. "Nothing lasts, Angel. You will be married soon, as will Rowena."

Lady Rowena Gresham, who paced restlessly as she cast a knowing eye at the crops in a neighbouring field, took one last bite of her apple and threw the core at Melisende, hitting her squarely on the back. "Hush, Melly, I was happy until you said that. I'll never marry, unlike Angel, lying there grinning like a fool while she dreams of a certain knight. And unlike you, marrying God." She folded her arms and looked upon the castle with a proprietorial air. "I will live here at Gresham, will run the castle, just as father does. And will live happily ever after."

"'Tis that simple?" Angelique's grin broadened at the sight of Rowena's supremely confident stance, and turned into laughter as she met Melisende's answering smile. But Rowena didn't laugh, just looked out at the line of darkness that lay on the northern horizon. Melisende was right. A change was coming…

Claiming
Book 1—Rowena

.

CHAPTER ONE

Gresham Castle, Norfolk, England, 1207

Lady Rowena Gresham rode alone, ahead of her men as usual, along the well-worn bridle path that led to Gresham Castle. The crop of barley she'd been inspecting barely moved under the hot summer sun, but it wasn't the bright light that made her eyes burn.

She swallowed hard, trying to keep at bay the knot of grief that would not release its grip. Her beloved father was dead and she doubted the pain of his loss would ever leave. She'd held him in her arms and watched him slip away from her, hour by hour, minute by minute, until his hands had gone limp in hers.

If that wasn't enough she'd now been summonsed back to her own castle, by the High Sheriff of Norfolk and Suffolk no less. His name sent a frisson of fear through her body. There had been no word from her father's liege lord, and now the sheriff had arrived, unannounced. It did not bode well.

She urged her horse to the top of the ridge that overlooked the fertile river valley in which her castle lay, and reined him in sharply. Below her dozens of strangers swarmed around the castle bailey, disrupting the usual ebb and flow of people going about their business. The sheriff was not alone.

She frowned as the fear that had nagged in her head moved lower, gripping her gut. She spurred her horse into a gallop. The estate was *hers*, *hers*. *Hers*, she repeated again and again in time to the beat of her heart and the pounding of her stallion's hooves on the dry ground.

Rowena strode into the Great Hall, shadowy after the bright sunlight, followed closely by two greyhounds who loped subserviently behind her. Her attention was immediately focused on the two men who stood by the light of the great window—one was the sheriff, the other a priest. *Why, in God's name, had the sheriff brought a priest with him?*

"Sir William!" She beckoned to a servant to bring her wine. "I would offer you refreshment but I see you are both already enjoying my best Bordeaux. I hope it is to your liking?"

"Excellent, my lady." He glanced over her shoulder and then back to her, his expression hard, unreadable. "Please accept my condolences on the death of your father. He was a good man."

She shrugged. Of all the things her father could be called, "good" wasn't one of them. He was strong, brave and could outwit his wiliest enemy, but he hadn't been "good". But she wasn't going to argue the point with strangers. "Thank you. Please, be seated." She accepted a goblet of wine from one of her servants and dropped down into a chair with a confidence she didn't feel.

She took a sip of the wine and carefully placed it on the table as her mind raced, trying to gain their measure. Despite her quickened heart beat, she sat back, laced her fingers together and held them before her as she focused intently on the men, waiting for them to crumple like men usually did before the "Gresham stare". She had inherited it from her father. Just like her personality, just like the estate.

"So, to what do I owe the pleasure of your visit?" She refused to call it a summons.

The grizzled-haired sheriff rubbed his lips in silent consideration, as his eyes narrowed against her insolence.

"You are like your father, my lady, inclined to the point."

"You compliment me, sir."

"No, my lady, I do not. However under the present circumstances such directness is useful. 'Twill save me time."

Rowena bit her lip. She'd angered him. It would not be wise to anger such a powerful man. She took a deep breath. "And these circumstances…?"

"Your father, my lady, was a wise man."

She nodded, feeling a slight lessening of the tension. Sir William was correct this time. "Indeed."

"And his estates have always been prosperous."

"He worked hard to make them so. We both did."

"Yes," Sir William looked at her with a cool, disapproving gaze. "I have heard of your unusual interest in the estate." His lips curled into a smile that sent a chill down her back. She shivered and one of the dogs leaned against her legs, sensing something was amiss. "You will no doubt be pleased to know you no longer have to run the estate alone."

Rowena gasped as if winded and bit her lip as she tried to hide her reaction to his words. She reached down to the dog and petted it, giving herself time to try to understand, try to cover her confusion.

"I know not what you mean, sir." She tried to form a smile as she looked up at Sir William, but she feared it hadn't worked because he was not smiling back at her.

"I mean, Lady Rowena, that your father's estate has now been settled and I'm here to advise you of this."

Rowena gripped the arm of the chair for strength, willing the fear and anger that raged inside not to emerge. "Settled? It is already settled. With due respect, my Lord, my father's wishes for the estate have been well known by everyone concerned for years. He has divided it between his three daughters, with Gresham Castle and its surrounding estates being my share."

Sir William did not reply immediately but a sly glimmer of a smile rested briefly on his lips before he took a sip of his wine, his steely gaze all the while focused on her. He was playing her. The bastard was making her suffer. But she would not show weakness before him. She reached across for her wine and took a small sip, replacing the goblet with the same deliberate control. She brought her hands loosely together and raised an eyebrow in query.

"Your liege lord has charged me with informing you that he agrees to your father's wishes. Your sisters do indeed inherit their portions as you say. But this estate? No. Your esteemed father has passed you over in favour of Sir Saher de Bohun. Sir Saher is now lord of Gresham Castle and its estates."

She didn't move a muscle. It was as if ice, crushed and made liquid, had been poured into her body. It felt an age she sat there as dismay, fear, and anger raged inside her.

It was only when Sir William finished his wine and gave her a smug smile that she rose and smiled back. She knew she smiled because she felt her lips curl. But she felt no smile within, only sickness.

"No. You must be mistaken. My father would never have done such a thing. Now, if you've quite finished I have business to attend. I have no time to listen to such tales." She turned to go, clicking her fingers to summon the dogs to her side.

"These are no tales, my lady." The unfamiliar deep voice echoed around the large space. She snapped her head around, searching the shadows for its owner.

"Who's there?"

He stepped forward from behind a screen, until his outline was illuminated by a halo of orange firelight. He looked like the devil himself.

7

"Lady Rowena," Sir William's voice had a smug tone which didn't go undetected. "Allow me to introduce Sir Saher de Bohun, Lord of Gresham. He is a relative of your father's."

Anger broke the chill. She looked him up and down. "Of course he is. It's surprising how many relatives emerge when a wealthy man dies."

Sir Saher came close to her, too close, but she refused to back away. Despite her own good height, he was at least a foot taller than her and broader built than any Gresham man. His skin was browned by the sun, his muscles hard and his eyes and jaw harder still. "Quite a performance, Lady Rowena. I'm impressed."

"Impressed? I have no need, nor wish, to impress you." She turned back to Sir William. "Who will vouch that he is who he says he is?"

"None other than your liege lord, the Earl of Norfolk, Lady Rowena, and the King himself. There is no doubt. Sir Saher has been on the King's business these past few years and is now here on his own business. Sir Saher is lord and master of Gresham Castle and its estates. And *that*, my lady, is fact. Your liege lord anticipated you might be... unaccepting, shall we say, and requested that I ensure the peaceful handover. And now that has been accomplished, we will take your leave."

"There will be no peaceful handover. There will be no handover at all. The land is mine."

Saher raised an eyebrow and his hard grey eyes—the colour of flint— sparked with amusement. "You exceed your reputation, lady. I'd heard that you are your father's daughter, but I had imagined some softening of his character."

"You imagined wrong. You'll not be taking my place as head of this estate. *I* am in charge and always will be. I suggest you leave immediately."

The smiled broadened, the lines around his eyes crinkling into an intensely irritating smile. "Now why would I do that, when I've only just arrived? Be seated, lady, and listen."

"I do not take orders from anyone, sir. Least of all in my own Hall."

"Priest," Sir William interrupted. "Pass Lady Rowena the scroll. Let her see with her own eyes her father's wishes and those of the Earl and King, and have done with this nonsense."

The priest, who'd been nervously holding a scroll in his ink-stained hands, unrolled it and passed it to her. "It says—"

She snatched it from him. "I can read." She scanned the parchment, confusion building with each passing word. She stopped abruptly when she saw her father's distinctive signature. It was his hand. Betrayal, sickening and lurid, filled her stomach. She turned slowly to this man, this stranger, this barbarian, and took the document and tore it in half. The rending of the precious scroll shocked the observers into silence. She looked from one to the other of them. "This is what I think of the document. Whatever my

8

father did, or did not do, I own the estate and I run the estate. And as to the rest, it will never happen."

The tall stranger clapped his hands slowly. "Brave, but foolish words. We have other copies of the document." He came towards her, towering over her, trying to intimidate her but she refused to move. "And it *will* happen."

"You seem to forget to whom you speak, sir."

"I know exactly to whom I speak. I would not mistake the woman whose father left his entire estate—including her—to me.

"What?"

"Yes. Your father not only left me his land, manors and castles. He left me *you*. We are to be married, my lady."

CHAPTER TWO

Rowena pressed her hand to her side, trying to stem the pain and panic that swamped her. She could hardly believe it—after all these years of being her father's closest daughter, to have worked and lived alongside him, for him to then betray her in this manner? They must be wrong.

"You are mad, sir."

He huffed quietly as if the idea amused him. "No. Despite a life that at times has driven me close to it, I am not mad." He beckoned to the priest. "Certainly sane enough to ensure that the highest authority in the county," he nodded respectfully to Sir William, "witnesses our betrothal ceremony."

It was too much. She paced away from the fire, and looked out the unshuttered window to the busy bailey. Sir Saher's men were everywhere, commandeering stables, her own people doing as they were bid as if she'd already lost control. She gritted her teeth—she had to fight for this. She turned to him, her hands seeking out the hard, cold stone to stop herself from showing weakness. "You speak of marriage, of being my father's heir, yet I have no knowledge of your existence before now."

"Your knowledge, my lady," interjected the sheriff curtly, "is not important."

Rowena ignored the sheriff's comment and continued to look accusingly at the man who was to be her husband. "It is to me." The sheriff huffed angrily and paced away.

"'Tis fitting for Lady Rowena to know." Saher answered smoothly. "My lady mother was a cousin of your father's."

"No doubt he had many cousins. Why you?"

"I fought with him in France. We got to know each other well and he spoke of you often. He wanted you to stay on this land, to be safe on this land."

She turned away then, as she felt the pain shoot through her body and come to rest in her head, pressing against her skull. She closed her eyes tight. Her father knew her. He knew that the land was the most important thing to her. Nothing else. She'd always been her father's favourite child, but he'd betrayed her. Her mind raced to comprehend the choices available to her. There were only two—she could either stay on the lands she loved and marry this man, or she could leave. But she refused to leave destitute, with no options. No. She had to keep her cool, had to think.

She took a long deep breath and turned back to the men.

"Let me get this straight. My father has bequeathed the estate to you, providing you will marry me. And the King agrees to this ridiculous arrangement. What if I decline?"

"I will still inherit the estate and you will have nothing."

The truth of his words slammed into her gut. "You cannot want to marry me."

"I wish to have heirs. You are as good as anyone else."

"Charming."

"I'm not known for my charm."

"I'm not surprised. I dare say you are *not* known for many things."

He came around her then and flicked away some barley seeds that had caught in a strand of hair that had escaped her coif. "Do not try to insult me, lady. For one thing, I am immune to insults, and for another, it gives you a distinct unladylike quality."

She slapped his hand away. "I care nought for your opinion. There is only one man whose opinion I regarded"—she turned away—"and he is now dead."

She sensed him behind her. "You really believed you would inherit the estate, didn't you?" His tone was softer now.

"Of course. It was always understood that that was what would happen."

"He told you this?"

"He…" She couldn't continue because as her memory roamed back and forth over the years she'd spent time with her beloved father, those words had never passed his lips. "He made it known."

"But not through words. My lady, he could never have left you this land. If he loved you, he would never have left you undefended. These are troubled times, no one and nothing is safe, least of all an estate as wealthy as this one."

"I could have defended it." Rowena was annoyed to hear her voice catch.

"You, with your great knowledge of defence and warfare?"

She turned to him then, her eyes glinting with unshed tears and barely suppressed rage. "I know my castle, I know my land, I know my people. *That* is enough."

"Your father knew it wasn't and entrusted me with the care of the castle and of you. Besides, even if he had been of a mind to leave it all to you, his liege lord would never have let such a prize be awarded without his involvement. Upon your father's death, you became his responsibility. You must have known this."

She tried to speak but couldn't for he spoke the truth.

"You knew it, but found it convenient to forget it, to believe otherwise."

"I know my liege lord. He would have been content enough to carry on collecting the revenue from our lands. He knew I could continue to produce it. He obviously changed his mind. You, sir, changed it for him. How much did you have to pay to make him agree?"

"Enough."

She closed her eyes, trying desperately to regain control of her life, of her thoughts... But she opened her eyes and the man still loomed tall over her, dominating her. But, beneath it all, her sense of betrayal ground into the pit of her stomach, undermining everything. "How did you know my father? How did you make him do such a thing to me?"

She saw a flicker of reaction in his grey eyes that warmed and swept his features as if he was, himself, frustrated. He turned to the sheriff. "Sir William. Lady Rowena accepts the terms of the will, as do I." He turned back to her. "Don't you?"

She nodded stiffly.

"I have a financial settlement drafted if you care to look at it."

"I care all right." She took the document and read through it. If he should die she'd be well cared for—the dower package was generous. She looked up at him and nodded. "'Tis satisfactory."

"Good. Sir William, I would have the betrothal ceremony witnessed before you leave." He glanced at Rowena. "So everyone will know the Lady Rowena has consented, that our marriage will be legal... once consummated." He reached for her hand but she stepped away, putting both hands behind her back. He shrugged. "I take you as my wife. Do you wish to take me as your husband?"

Rowena tried to speak but her mouth was dry with shock. She took a deep breath and swallowed, holding her head high. "If I have to."

"If you wish to stay here, you do."

"Then I will take you as my husband."

He took her right hand and this time she didn't withdraw it. She had no alternative but to suffer his large, calloused hand wrapping around, and dwarfing, hers. He looked at her sharply, obviously aware of the tremor in her hand. "I take you as my wife, for better or worse, to have and to hold until the end of my life and of this I give you my faith." He bent toward her. "Come, lady, say the words and it will be over."

Then he squeezed her hand, his thumb sweeping over the back of her hand in a gesture of compassion that startled her. She gazed up into his eyes and knew she had no option but to continue. "I take you as my husband, to have and to hold until the end of my life and of this…" Her voice cracked and she cleared her throat. "I give you my faith."

He dropped her hand, taking away his warmth and careless gesture, bringing her back to reality. "Good." He turned to Sir William. "Thank you, Sir William, for your help in this matter.

"You are most welcome, my lord, and congratulations on your good fortune. As to the marriage, there will be no need to issue bans, or for a ceremony at the church door. It is sufficient that we have witnessed it on behalf of the King. No-one dare gainsay it. All you have to do now, sir, to complete the deal, is to consummate it." He glanced at Rowena and returned an amused look back to Saher. "Good luck with that."

Saher ignored the innuendo. "Are you sure you don't wish to stay for more refreshment?"

"I must return to Norwich. I wish you well in your new endeavours." He turned to Rowena. "My lady, I wish you well, also. No matter what you think, your father sought the best for you. I suggest you make the best of it."

Rowena nodded coolly. "I intend to, sir."

Sir William gave a pointed glance at Sir Saher. "Good luck, sir, I think you're going to need it."

She walked away from them, hoping that Sir Saher would leave also. She poured herself more wine and sipped it with her back to the door. Suddenly there was silence. She waited, her ears acute, listening for the slightest sound, hoping against hope that she was now alone. But then she heard his footfall approach her. She closed her eyes once more.

"I made your father do nothing, my lady. I spent many months with him five years ago, in France. He was a tough man with a hard heart. He did nothing on a whim. He knew me well, knew what I sought, and believed I could be of use to him. And of use to you."

"And what is it that you seek?"

"Lands, a wife, children."

She pressed her hand flat against her chest, trying to come to terms, now, with the idea of lying with this stranger. It was unthinkable. She'd lain with a man years before and had had her heart broken. She'd vowed then and there to never allow herself to be vulnerable again, to allow the needs of her body to lead her to destruction. She'd fought off any suitors, much to her father's amusement. And he'd let her. All the while knowing that he planned her marriage after his death. It had been *convenient* for him to have the attentions of the daughter with whom he was closest. That was all.

She took a deep breath. "Well, you have the first two on your list. Do you care to make a start on the last item? The solar is empty. You could throw me over your shoulder and take me to bed, now. No-one would know. In fact, forget the bed, pull up my robe now and be done with it."

He sighed, strode up to her and gripped her arms. His fingers dug into her skin but she refused to look away from him, or to flinch. He dipped his head to hers. "Now, *that* is an idea." His breath was unexpectedly warm and pleasant against her cheek and sent a ripple of sensation across her skin that travelled beyond where his breath touched her. She widened her eyes, suddenly alarmed, suddenly out of her depth, suddenly aware that he'd noticed her reaction. His lips upturned into a slow smile as he swept a finger along her jaw line. "I was wrong. Your softness isn't in your heart— there, you are like your father—it is in your body. You think you don't want me, you believe you are impervious to men—you are mistaken."

She didn't move. She *couldn't* move. Her whole body was held in thrall by the stray touch of his hand on her face. It was as if his touch delved deep into her body, like the last quivering note of a lute, designed to transport the heart to a different place. Then he withdrew his touch and the magic was broken. She stepped away, feeling as if she'd drunk too much of the Bordeaux.

"I think... I think, I should know my own *mind*, my own *heart*, my own *body*."

"Aye, but you don't." His finger insolently stole round her neck and she gasped. "Do you? Look at how the blush creeps up your neck and fills your cheeks. At how your breath quickens and the indentation in your neck flutters." He shifted his hand up until it rested on a hollow and she felt the quickened movement under his fingertips. "Just here. You are not immune to me in the least. You want me. And you shall have me."

She brought her arm up and pushed his away. "I will not. Go, sir. Go now. Leave me at once."

"I will not be leaving here, my lady. Didn't you hear Sir William? I just need to bed you and we will be married."

"Then we shall never be married because I will not sleep with you. I will never lie with you, never have your children."

"Listen here, lady. We *will* live together, we *will* sleep together and everyone *will* believe we have lain together. It will be enough for others. But for me? No. I will not leave you until I've bedded you."

"You would not force yourself on me?"

"I won't have to. I've plenty of experience with women. I know an aroused woman when I see one. I know the look of a woman whose eyes explore the lips of a man she wishes to kiss and whose thoughts stray to a man's body, wondering and wanting."

She swallowed and forced a low laugh. "I'm sure you would believe every woman wishes to bed you. However, in my case, your knowledge has proved faulty. I would sooner bed an adder; I would sooner lie in the filth of an animal's pen; I would sooner kiss a leper."

He smiled. "I knew this wouldn't be easy, but, by the Lord, I had no idea it would be such entertainment."

Before she could reply, he'd slipped his hand around her head and pressed his lips against hers in a kiss designed to dominate. But his breathing quickened, his lips moved as though he wanted to explore hers, and a groan of pleasure, ran through his body, under her hands that were pressed against his chest, ready to push him away. Ready... but not pushing.

For one long moment neither of them moved. Then a shout from outside brought them both to their senses. She raised her hands from his unyielding chest and slapped his face.

"How dare you, sir." She stepped away, horrified at his response... and hers.

"I dare many things, my lady wife. But I'm not in the habit of pressing myself on women who don't want me. It won't happen again." He turned away, and walked to the door where he hesitated and turned once more to her. "Until you instigate it yourself, that is."

"Then it will never happen," she spat out.

The door slammed shut on her. And she was glad that he was no longer there to witness the vivid colour that had spread over her cheeks, the shaking hand that she pressed against her hot lips, and the panting breath that refused to subside.

She staggered back into a chair and put her head in her hands. What was happening to her? In one afternoon, she'd had that which she valued most—her home—taken from her, and that which she feared the most—the passionate nature she'd inherited from her mother, revealed to her. It couldn't be. It *mustn't* be. She refused to succumb to such a passion. It had been her mother's undoing. It would *not* be hers.

CHAPTER THREE

Rowena scowled as she looked around the hall from her position at the raised table, and skewered another piece of meat from her trencher.

She'd been over and over her predicament in her mind, trying to find a way to rid herself of this man, to reclaim her lands and herself. But there was none. Sir Saher not only inherited her father's estate legally, but he also held it in fact. His men were fighters, hers were farmers and there was no-one willing to gainsay either the Earl of Norfolk or the King, no-one to defend her lands or herself. Her father's "friends" hadn't answered her urgent request for help, no doubt preferring to have Saher as their protector rather than a weak woman.

She was no match for him. She could leave. But where would she go, on her own, without money? She would have nothing. To one of the suitors she'd rejected in the past? Even if she could get one of the few who remained unmarried to marry her, and persuade them to fight for what was rightfully hers, she'd be no better off than she was now.

She refreshed her goblet and sat back in the chair with a sigh. She could go and join Melisende and her aunt, the Abbess, at Blakesmere Priory. It wasn't a life she wanted for herself but she'd go if she had to, and take her money with her. Her aunt and sister were the only people she could trust with her money. It would be safe there.

Rowena glanced at Saher who was questioning her steward on the estate's accounts. She hoped her steward had done as she'd instructed and hidden well the money which was hers—and would stay hers—alone. She had to bite her lip to stop herself from interrupting. It would only make it appear she had something to hide, which she had. Silver—which she was due to collect from the Flemish merchant, with whom her father had secret business, on the morrow. Some called such business smuggling, but in these times of heavy taxes, her father had called it prudent. It would be enough to buy her a future with the Priory should she ever need it. She just needed Saher gone so she could collect the casks of coin from the merchant and deliver them safely to the Priory. But how to rid herself of this unwanted husband who'd made himself so at ease in her own castle?

Saher turned and dipped his head to her ear, so he could be heard over the raucous laughter and noise in the Hall. "You are looking thoughtful, my lady. Considering what names to call our children?"

She wanted to ignore him but he was too provoking. "'Tis blasphemous, sir, to suggest I could bear a child without having done the necessary deed to produce it. You liken me to a lady to whom no mortal could aspire."

His laugh was loud and filled the Great Hall. "Least of all you. The Blessed Virgin would be the last person I would liken you to."

She looked around quickly. "Hush, 'tis rowdy talk."

He leaned forward. "And you don't like rowdy talk?"

"'Tis not appropriate only days after my father's burial."

He placed his goblet thoughtfully onto the table. "Ah yes, your father. His sudden passing must have been a shock to you."

Rowena glanced at his face but found him to be serious and turned away sharply, narrowing her eyes as if she was looking for someone, trying to cover the swell of mixed emotions his words evoked.

She cleared her throat. "Indeed. I had imagined he would live a long life. But 'twas not to be."

She felt his eyes suddenly upon her and wondered for a moment if he could detect the pain that gave a slight tremor to her words. But he couldn't have done, for he looked away just as quickly.

"You were his great companion, I understand."

She hesitated before she spoke, as her mind turned back to her beloved father. "Yes, we enjoyed each other's company. I gave him due respect and love and he gave me free rein around the estate and castle." She bit her lip as she felt the pain in her heart that her father's passing had left. She cleared her throat and blinked. "The fire is exceptionally smoky tonight." She signalled to an attendant to add more wood. Although it was summer, the nights were chill and the Hall was large.

"Free rein? I think not. While he was alive to watch over you, you had your *supposed* freedom. But he knew, full well, that you and the estates needed protection after his death. And you must have known, too, that your father would choose a husband for you."

She shook her head. "He tried once or twice, of course, but I refused." She shrugged. "I have no interest in men."

"Now *that*, I do not believe. Maybe you were put off men for one reason or another, but I do not believe you had no interest." His eyes narrowed.

"You have passion in your eyes. I can feel it, I can see it. What went wrong?"

How could he have guessed so accurately? A vision of the young man who had stolen her heart and her virginity flashed into her mind. She'd been fifteen—too young, too impetuous and too easily fooled by a few flirtatious words and flattery. Another woman—older and wealthier than she—had beckoned to him and he'd gone. Sold to the highest bidder. She'd decided there and then that she would never again fall prey to the appetites of her body, appetites that had also been her mother's downfall.

She shrugged in what she hoped was a casual manner. "My past is none of your business."

"True. But I'd always found understanding people helped greatly in everything I do."

"Everything? You are a mercenary, are you not? So understanding people helped you to murder them?"

"*Was* a mercenary."

"You still are sir. You've sold your services to the highest bidder, as before. My lord father must have thought it a great joke, to match me up with you." She didn't even try to keep the bitterness out of her voice.

"He knew that I could guard and protect you and his lands like no other man could."

"Strange form of protection—gifting my life to a stranger."

"Better than gifting to you a life of certain defeat and ignominy."

She placed her wine goblet carefully on the table, trying not to spill the ruby liquid, trying not to reveal the fact that she feared he spoke the truth. "Nothing is certain, my lord. Not defeat, not ignominy. Only death."

"Come now. You are too young and beautiful to contemplate death."

She glanced at the rapidly reducing wine flagon. "The wine is obviously addling your eyes and brains. I am too old to be considered young."

"You consider twenty-one years of age, old?"

"You know it is. All my friends were married by the time they were eighteen, or earlier. And, as to your other point, I have too healthy a complexion and body to be considered beautiful."

His eyes travelled leisurely down her curves. She met his gaze with a narrowed one of her own. "I see nought to complain about."

She leaned toward him, as if to speak confidentially. "How ill you are at the gentle art of wooing, my lord. Because, even to me, unused to such talk, 'nought to complain about' is seldom used to flatter a lady."

"Indeed, you have me there." Even under the intermittent flicker of the torchlight, Rowena could see the unmistakable flare of interest in his eyes. Eyes that had grown darker with each passing moment. "While I hardly think I need to woo my wife, all this talk of beauty makes me think that you desire me to court you."

"That's…" she spluttered, "that's utterly ridiculous. I have no wish to be courted."

"Just bedded and married then?"

"Certainly no wish for either of these."

"The last of these has been accomplished but I can add in some wooing if it sweetens the idea of being bedded. You are obviously acquainted with the art of wooing for you to criticize my efforts—"

"Not at all—"

"Tell me, what words should I be using?"

"I have no interest in such matters. You purposely misunderstand."

"Your protestations simply convince me further of my rightness."

"So… if I speak, you disbelieve me, and if I say nothing, I cannot defend myself."

"*That* is about the sum of it."

"Then I shall save myself the bother of conversing." Rowena rose. "I'll bid you goodnight, sir. Do not even think to disturb me."

"You seem to forget, lady, that we share the same solar."

"You touch me and—"

"You would enjoy it, believe me."

"You would not force me?"

"You're right. I would not. I never have, and I never will, force a woman into my bed—the thought is abhorrent to me. But I will lie close to you, watching you, but not touching you. And then there's tomorrow. Tomorrow, 'twill be different." He looked at her thoughtfully. "Tomorrow we will begin our courtship."

A thrill of excitement shot through her, as she remembered his lips against hers. She couldn't risk being close to him, couldn't risk being weakened by lust. "Surely you have better things to do."

"Aye. I have. We can inspect the estates together. Tomorrow, show me the estate's business at the port. Seduce me with your words of business and I'll seduce you with my words of love."

"You're wasting your time. Instead of seduction you should be about your business."

"As of today, seduction is my business. And I'm going nowhere until you come to me willingly." The noise she uttered made him laugh. "Go to bed, sweetheart, gather your strength. You'll be needing it."

Rowena gritted her teeth at his arrogance but did not reply. She didn't trust herself. Instead she walked away without a backward glance, calling to her maid who was laughingly fighting off the attentions of one of Saher's men.

It certainly wasn't the heat of the fire that enflamed her cheeks and her body now, but anger at finding her freedom curtailed. Nothing else. Certainly nothing to do with the hot lick of desire his touch, his words and his eyes had sparked. Certainly nothing to do with the knowledge that there was clearly only one way to get him to leave the castle—to allow herself to be seduced by him.

CHAPTER FOUR

"'Tis too dark to see in this small room, my lady," Birghiva muttered as she opened the shutters to let in what little light there was, before returning to fuss over Rowena's hair.

Rowena's gaze was immediately drawn to the faint outline of the deserted tower on top of the hill, barely visible in the pre-dawn light. Despite her dread of the place and the memories it held for her, her gaze was inevitably drawn to it, a constant reminder of what could happen to a woman.

"Turn to me, my lady, I cannot dress your hair if you insist on twisting around."

"Keep your voice down, Birghiva. I don't want Sir Saher awakened."

"You look tired, my lady," she whispered.

Rowena knew the question Birghiva wanted to ask, but she wasn't of a mind to answer it. Let people think what they wished. For, if people thought she hadn't lain with Saher, that they weren't properly married, then it could be the worse for her—Saher could expel her from the castle on any grounds whatsoever. She sighed. "So would you be."

Birghiva raised an amused eyebrow. She wasn't to know that the cause of Rowena's tiredness was the fact she'd lain awake all night watching the man who was her husband. At least he'd taken the hint and slept on the pallet she'd placed on the floor for him. She felt as if she'd lain the whole night watching the course of the moon track across the room, illuminating his body, his hair, the rise and fall of his chest. The light brought form to his face, form to her fate. She supposed she must have dozed as some point but she'd been awake and arisen before him. And she wanted to be away on her business before him. He might want time together. But she most certainly did not. She had a merchant to meet and illicit funds to receive, neither of which she wanted the king's man to witness.

"There," Birghiva patted Rowena's hair and stepped away. "That should do it."

Rowena fastened the silver clasp of her cloak around her, glad of the cloak's warmth in the chill of the summer morning. "Your cloak, Birghiva. Come, we mustn't delay."

Birghiva swiftly obeyed. "Aye." She swept it around her shoulders. "Although why you don't wait for Sir Saher, I don't know."

"Because I don't wish to be with him. He may be my husband but he is not, and never will be, my keeper."

She took one last look out the window at the jagged edged tower—a symbol of everything she feared—and silently pushed open the door and slipped past the solar where Saher lay.

Rowena looked up from the clerk's figures with satisfaction. They accounted for the goods currently being loaded onto her ship—a fine cog, bigger than the others that were tied up beside it at the quay. A line of men carried the cargo aboard—grain, hides and wool destined for Germany— that made her estates so profitable. She inhaled the unique port smell of salt air, rank mud and the fragrant food from the nearby Inn and stalls that lined the road. She glanced at the sun. It would soon be time for her meeting with the Flemish merchant to arrange the next shipment and collect payment on the last. She was relieved she'd managed to evade Sir Saher. He would ask awkward questions, questions she couldn't answer honestly, not if she wanted an escape route.

"Good morning, my lady."

Rowena jumped at the whispered greeting, close to her ear, and blushed, as if caught red-handed, wondering if her thoughts hadn't somehow summoned him to her. She recovered quickly and gave him a cool stare which seemed to amuse him.

"Sir Saher! I did not expect to see you here." She was suddenly nervous, aware of what her father's reaction to her disobedience would have been. But, strangely, his expression was not one of anger.

"And I didn't expect to be here, my lady, I assure you. What I expected was to break my fast in a leisurely fashion and to be shown around the estates by my wife and steward. Not chase around the countryside after my wife."

"It just shows that life seldom gives us what we expect. Now, if you'll excuse me, I have business to attend."

She turned away and walked along the wooden planks placed on top of the mud for the men loading the cargo. She'd hoped he'd take the not-so-subtle hint and leave, but he fell into step beside her.

"Excellent idea. I'll join you and you can show me the Gresham holdings while I am here. Let's not make it a total waste of a morning." Her heart sank. How was she going to lose Sir Saher before she met up with the merchant? "This vessel is very fine," he indicated the large cog before them.

"The finest." She stopped walking and looked up at the ship proudly. "It can sail all around Cape Skagen to get to the Baltic, with no ill effect. And the fore and stern castles, which you see we've added, are the best defence against pirates. Our trade with the Baltic and Germany is flourishing because of it. The merchants will take as much grain as we can produce."

"Excellent. I can see the estate's business is in good hands."

She turned to him in surprise. "You would leave it to me, sir?" She could barely hope that such a man as this would allow his wife any authority.

She jumped as he reached out and took her hands in his. "These hands are capable, I've no doubt, but do not think I allow you complete control over the estate's affairs, for I do not. I will be looking through the accounts later today and I expect you to inform me of all I need to know." She wanted to pull back her hands from his but she was frozen, aware only of the gentle way he held her, and of its effect on her. She swallowed and held his gaze, waiting with a heightened sense of anticipation to see what he would do next. He smiled. "Now, lead on, show me the Gresham warehouse I've heard so much about."

She did as he bid, not least so she didn't have to look into those dark grey eyes that seemed to see directly into the heart of her. She shook her head in a vain attempt to rid it of the confusion brought about by his touch and words, and stopped beside open warehouse doors from which a stream of men laden with cargo emerged.

"The Gresham warehouse. We keep the goods here until the cog has returned. My father employed learned men to advise on its construction and the goods therefore keep well and are sought-after because of it. We keep a mix of..." She blushed, suddenly realizing she was getting carried away with her enthusiasm for the subject. She waved her arm. "I'm talking too much, I'm sure you're not interested. Few people are. But it's what has made us prosperous in bad times."

A smile flickered on his lips, as though he found her passion amusing. "Impressive," but he was looking at her. "A fighter and a businesswoman."

"My father taught me to take care of business. He taught me to look out for myself, to not trust others."

"These are good lessons. But you know, Lady Rowena, he trusted *me* with his most beloved possession. Should you not also?"

There was a heavy pause and she couldn't prevent herself from frowning as the truth of his words hit home. She'd loved her father, despite his many faults. Not least of which was the imprisonment of her mother, a woman whose unbalanced and passionate nature had been her downfall. But he had always been mistrustful of people, except obviously, of this man. Should she trust him?

She only knew it was too soon, she knew him too little. Besides it wasn't in men's *words* that she could trust—she knew *that* through experience—it was in their actions.

"You must have business of your own, sir. I am merely meeting a merchant to discuss a further shipment." She waved her hand in what she hoped was an airy, unconcerned fashion. "'Tis nothing important, too small to interest you."

"Believe me, my lady. I am very interested in all your business." He narrowed his eyes. "And I doubt very much 'tis 'small.'"

Rowena turned away, and drew in a sharp, anxious breath, and walked into the shadowy interior of the warehouse where she knew the merchant secretly awaited her.

She walked past the barrels and pallets, most of which contained grain bound for Germany, but still others with goods bound for Iceland and the Baltic countries. She hoped the smell of the dried fish awaiting despatch to various English ports would put Saher off but no, his footsteps followed her, echoing on the dusty wooden floors.

She indicated to her steward, who was looking nervously on, to do something.

"Sir Saher!" he called. "Last night you mentioned your interest in the French wine we are importing. Do you care for a taste of our most recent imports? 'Tis the best."

Saher looked from Rowena, to her steward and then back to Rowena again. "It seems, my lady, your men are loyal. I'll go now. But I'll return in a few moments."

As soon as Saher had walked out into the bright sunshine, Rowena moved quickly to the rear door where she was met by the merchant. Accustomed to transacting their business discreetly and swiftly, the negotiations were soon complete. He'd indicated which casks, amongst the many, contained the coins and now all Rowena had to do was somehow remove them securely from here and deposit them at the Priory. Her hopes for the future depended on it.

Within moments the merchant had stepped towards the door but hadn't reached it when she heard the steward's voice rising in warning. She turned as Saher bore down on her. He tried to look over her shoulder and there was nothing else for it—she knew the merchant had yet to leave the warehouse—and she grabbed Saher's hand and clasped it tight between her own. He turned sharply towards her.

"My lady? What is the matter?"

"The matter?" Rowena's mind raced as she tried to think of something, anything, that would prevent him from discovering the merchant, so obviously Flemish, so obviously flouting the law. "I... I've been thinking about what you said... about," she cleared her throat, "us..."

Concern was replaced by suspicion. "Us?"

A quick glance over his shoulder revealed the merchant frozen into inaction, unwilling to open the door and be revealed in the sudden blast of daylight. She had to do something and something fast. Without thinking further she stood on tip-toes and pressed her lips to Saher's.

She closed her eyes as his lips instantly responded with a pressure of their own, claiming her mouth with a sensuous caress that sent shivers of desire through her body. Neither moved for shocked moments, simply focused on the pressure of their lips against each others, in a kiss which held the rest of the world at bay. The raucous shouts and cries of the town outside the warehouse faded away; the pungent smells of the warehouse were replaced by the fresh outdoors smell of Saher's skin. The rough texture of his woollen cloak over which her hands had curled, was more dominant in her mind than the casks of coin beside which they stood.

She may have taken the initiative, but it was he who now took control. With a sharp intake of breath, he drew her body tight against his, his hands fanning around her waist, back and lower. At the same time, his lips explored hers as if savouring the sweetest delicacy. She felt his low rumble of pleasure against her mouth, intensifying the breathless tension that coiled deep inside of her.

The kiss must have lasted moments only, but when he pulled away from her and caressed her cheek briefly with his hand, she could have sworn more than seconds had past. She felt different. Her hands continued to hold on to him, as if wanting to prolong the connection that seemed to penetrate deeper than their skin.

"Interesting," he murmured. "Very interesting."

He stepped away and her hands fell, almost reluctantly by her sides. She took a deep breath, trying to quiet her breathing but she felt weak and gripped the edge of a barrel for support. "Interesting," she repeated raggedly. It wasn't an adequate word for what had just passed between them but it was surely a safe one. She tried to regain her focus, tried to think, but nothing made sense apart from an overwhelming need to have those same lips, that same body, pressed tight against hers once more.

It was only when she heard the calls of the porters outside the warehouse that she dragged in a deep breath of pungent stale air and remembered where she was, remembered the contents of the heavy cask upon which her hand rested. The weight of freedom.

She glanced over his shoulder, the merchant had disappeared. "And now," she cleared her throat to try to make her voice less husky. "I think we'd better return to the castle."

"Indeed." He glanced at her briefly, frowning as if he was also trying to understand what had just passed between them.

She, too, was trying to understand. It was a kiss, yes, but nothing like the few she'd experienced before. Not even like the kiss he'd given her the day before. *That* had been all about domination. But this kiss? It didn't dominate and destroy, it created sensations that consumed all thought.

He cleared his throat and looked out through the open doors of the warehouse to the light and busy street beyond, as if searching to ground himself in reality again. "Although I can't say I've not enjoyed this... interlude, but your steward is waiting patiently for us to taste the wine and then, afterwards, I would like you to show me the estate."

She brought the cloak tightly around her and stepped hesitantly forward from behind the huge barrels that had sheltered them from view. "Of course."

She walked beside him to her steward who'd poured out three goblets of the latest import of wine from France and accepted one of them. She glanced up at Saher, suddenly shy, but he stood with the brightness of the open door behind him and she couldn't see the expression on his face. She glanced away and sipped her wine. Leaving him discussing the wine with her steward, she walked outside, needing to be grounded in the reality of the world.

She watched the plodding horses pull their heavy loads through the muddy street, the cluster of men—merchants and free workers alike—sup ale at the alehouse across the road, and the women call to their neighbours from the doorways of their tiny cottages that tumbled down the hill from the church, around the green, following the road to the quayside.

This was the real world, she chided herself. Where survival was difficult and vigilance was required. Not that other one she'd briefly experienced within the warehouse. That had been but a kiss. Only a kiss. To lose her wits because of it would surely be fatal. She couldn't be weak, as her mother had been. Her passion had led to her banishment from the castle, her banishment from her children and ultimate confinement to the tower. She glanced up at the tower that was visible for miles around. *That* had been her mother's fate. It would not be hers.

"My lady?" She turned to see Saher holding their horses. "Come. I would see what else lies in store for me. This day is proving more interesting than I had imagined."

Rowena's glanced at the casks that represented her freedom, checked that the extra guards she and her steward had ordered were in place and then nodded coolly in agreement to Saher. "Of course."

CHAPTER FIVE

Saher's gaze swept the crowded hall where wine and ale flowed and the best of food was available for all. The minstrels sang, the lights were bright and, for the first time in many a long year, he felt content. At last, his own castle and estate. He'd imagined he'd have felt easier. And he would have done if it hadn't been for Rowena's displeasure. Such marriages were made every day. If it had not been him, it would have been someone else, someone like Angelique's husband. On their ride home, Rowena had told him about her sisters, about her youngest, Melisende, at Blakesmere Priory, and about Angelique, forced into marriage to a man she despised and whom Rowena believed to be cruel. The thought of a man mistreating a woman made his blood boil and he took a soothing drink of wine and sat back, watching Rowena stretch across the table to reach her goblet.

He marvelled at the fact that most of the day's pleasure had been gleaned not from the estates, which were impressive, but from this woman. He watched as her sleeve fell back revealing an arm tanned on top, with a pale, delicate underside. The combination of the brown skin of her hands and arms, so disliked by noblewomen, with the white skin, so tender and vulnerable, did something to him. The tanned skin showed a strength and individuality that he admired. He hated weakness in anyone and had seen immediately that Rowena was a strong woman, a woman who could hold his attention and his desire. Then there was the delicacy of her pale, hidden skin, hinting at a vulnerability he longed to explore. He could only imagine how her passionate nature and bold mind would move that lush body once she'd discovered the joys he could bring to her. He hardened at the thought. And she was his for the taking anyway. Not that he would. He had the castle and its lands secure, and he would make his wife totally his, not

27

by taking, but by giving. That was the way with women. And that was the way with him. He'd not lied to her about his aversion to force when it came to women.

She shifted in her chair and he admired the long curve of her thigh. She said something that was hard to hear above the music and laughter in the hall and he shifted closer, until his thigh was pressed against hers. She stilled to begin with but didn't shift. The blush that rose through her body hardened him further as he imagined the effect on her breasts—full and heavy—just as he liked them.

She turned to him suddenly, her jaw lifted, its line strong and uncompromising in the flickering light. Her brown eyes flashed. She was a force to be reckoned with all right but he'd never been interested in meekness, not in animals, nor in women. She was like no other woman he'd ever wanted before, but he had to restrain himself, take her slowly, seduce her little by little. But, on second thoughts, maybe a little playful touching would not go amiss.

"I know not of what you are thinking, my lord, to make your hand stay, unwelcome on my thigh, or for your eyes to be so dark and penetrating."

"You are possibly better off not knowing."

"Is it so bad then?"

"No worse than any of my men who are enjoying themselves with your women."

"Yes." She looked around. "And my women seem not to dislike the attention."

"And why would they?" He clicked his fingers and the musicians began a number for dancing. Couples jumped up and began to form a circle.

"You dance, my lady?"

"No, I do not. My priest—thank the Lord he is not in attendance— would never allow it. Says it leads to unclean kissing."

He laughed. "I think all kissing is unclean to the church. But we are not at church and I'm all for dancing and kissing. Come." He stood and grabbed her hand. "I will show you how to dance."

People laughed to see the usually non-festive lady of the castle escorted, obviously unwillingly, onto the floor. She threw him a quick nervous glance and took hold of his outstretched hand, before turning and accepting the hand of the knight who stood to her left. People rushed to remove the trestle tables to give the dancers space, and they were soon shuffling, skipping and jumping in a circle as everyone joined the minstrels in singing the ronde.

Rowena tried to pull away from Saher's hand but he held it too firmly. He smiled to himself as he watched her try to retain her dignity and follow the other dancers. It didn't take long before he noticed a change in her. Slowly the pounding of the drum began to filter through the vibrations on the rush-strewn floor up into her body. He still gripped her hand, urging her to follow the dictates of her body, and she did—her movements becoming more fluid as she allowed only the rhythm of the drum and the harmony of the voices to enter her mind.

The ronde turned into another and another and still the dancers whirled, slowly slipping their hands away from the circle until only pairs of dancers twirled each other around, hair flying as clothing slipped out of place. When the music finally ceased, the Hall was wild with people hugging, laughing and singing. So no-one noticed when he led her out of the hall, toward the back chamber where they could have some privacy. She was out of breath and laughing as he slipped his arms around her waist and lifted her up against him. The laughing stilled as they both became aware of their bodies pressed against each others. Slowly he allowed her to slip down his body, until her feet were once more on the floor. He'd felt every slight movement of her rounded breasts against his chest, her sex against his before her stomach rested against his sex, arousing him further.

Beyond the chamber the music continued, growing more ribald. He shifted his hands so his thumbs could sweep the undersides of her breasts and lift them slightly. She gasped and he looked down at the thin muslin that barely covered them. Her nipples were just visible, as rosy as her lips, their points tight and hard.

She pulled away. "Enough, sir. We will be missed." She readjusted her gown and looked around.

"I very much doubt it. Listen, 'tis a night for merriment and… loving." So much for going slowly. He couldn't resist her.

She looked back at him then and he saw the tension in her eyes. She was as aroused as he was, but scared still. He placed his hands either side of her face and drew her close to him. He half-expected her to pull away but she didn't. He could see from her opened lips, her quickened breath and dark eyes that she wanted him. "Tell me when to stop, my lady, for I want to give you only what you wish to receive."

He hesitated but she made no sound, seemingly caught in a haze of expectation. He couldn't resist her softly plumped lips—parted and inviting—and he dipped his head to hers and kissed her. To his surprise she didn't stand immobile, but moved her mouth against his, while allowing his hands to caress her lush curves.

His whole body leaped at the meeting of their mouths and bodies, as if it'd come to life. It was like nothing he'd felt before. This was no barely satisfactory coupling, no fumbling desire to ease an itch. He could swear her passionate spirit was focused in her lips, communicating its strength and urgency to him, sparking into life a corresponding intensity and passion he thought had been subdued through the years of fighting and bloodshed. She breathed life into his darkness. And he wanted more.

He hadn't intended for this to be anything but a kiss, an indication to her of what was to come. But he couldn't stop himself from deepening the kiss. And she kissed him back with a wild abandon he'd sensed within her from the first. She pressed her body to his and opened her mouth wider to allow his tongue to explore hers. His hands slid down her back, caressing her shoulders, the sharp incline into the small of her back, and down further, onto the curves from which he'd been unable to take his eyes every time she turned her back to him. They were as luscious as he'd imagined. He spanned his fingers until they covered and tucked underneath those curves, drawing her into him.

She moaned under the ministrations of his hands, his tongue, his lips and without thinking, he lifted her and she slid her legs around his hips. She trembled in his arms—this strong warrior woman was vulnerable and needy for him. He groaned as his body heated and hardened under the knowledge of her surrender and his need for her—raw and unadulterated. He moved her back until she was pressed against the cold, flint wall, and ground his sex against hers. His lips sunk then to her neck, kissing and nipping as he went. Then the moon shifted from behind a cloud and showered its silvery light on the countryside, illuminating Rowena in its beams. She opened her eyes and looked out through the unshuttered window and froze. He drew back and followed her gaze out to the moon that illuminated the high ridge with its solitary tower that overlooked the castle, down to the fields that surrounded it. He turned to her once more, his heart was thumping, his mind and body narrowed to one purpose—possessing her.

She jammed her hands between their bodies and let her legs slide to the floor. She shook her head against his chest. He drew in a deep breath and let his hands fall.

"No, I can't, I don't want this," she said, shaking her head again and pursing her lips as if unable to say anything further. She looked up at him only briefly before picking up her skirts and running up the winding steps that led to her solar.

He hesitated a moment, trying to regain control over his body, trying to understand how such a passionate person as Rowena could have stopped the natural progression of their love-making. He didn't understand but, by God, he was going to. He followed her up the stairs.

The door was closed and he knocked. There was no answer so he pushed it open. "Rowena?"

She turned from the window where she was standing before the open shutters. She looked younger than her years, and vulnerable. "I thought..."

He stepped inside and closed the door. "You thought I would burst in on you whether you wished it or not? No, my lady, I don't do that. If you tell me to go, I will go. Do you?" She didn't answer but he saw the shake of her head in the moonlight. He went and stood behind her. "What is the matter, Rowena? Tell me what haunts you? What is it you're so afraid of?"

He put his hands gently on her shoulders and followed her line of vision, out beyond the shutters to the tower that stood atop the hill. It would have been used as a beacon in years past, but now it was a near ruin.

"I'm scared, Saher."

"You, scared? I don't believe you're afraid of anything."

"Oh, but I am."

"Tell me."

"I'm afraid of being claimed, being owned, and then," she turned away from the window to face him. "Of being abandoned. You must go… please." She placed her hands on his shoulders. He lifted her face to the moonlight and kissed her gently on the lips.

"I'll go, but you have no reason to fear being abandoned. Why would I? How could I? You are my wife. What is it really you afear? Is it that I'll turn into a brute like your sister's husband?"

She shook her head and looked out over the land, now flooded with moonlight, out to the broken-turreted tower. He followed her gaze. What was it that drew her attention so?

"Please go." Her voice was so uncharacteristically soft, so low, so plaintive that he could not bring himself to voice any words of objection.

Slowly, he thought to himself. He was meant to seduce her slowly. But his lust for her body had overridden his sense. He stepped away. "I don't know what you're hiding, Rowena, what fear that lies deep in your soul, but I will find it, I will eradicate it and I will claim you, heart and soul and body, to be mine."

"To do with as you wish?" Bitterness and fear edged her tone.

"To do with, as *you* wish. Not me. Because, believe me, you will want everything I have to offer. I can feel it on your skin, can hear it in your soft breath, as it pants into my ear, wanting me."

He walked away, down the corridor, down the narrow spiral stairs, back in to the heat and noise of the Hall. He settled himself by the fire with a goblet of wine and imagined Rowena, disrobing and lying on the fur throw in the moonlight, and of the things she'd beg him to do to her.

Rowena waited for Saher to return to their shared solar, awake and cursing the day that Saher had set foot inside the castle. It was a warm night and she could not sleep. The image of the tower haunted her. Captivity—it was the one thing she'd always feared, always thought her father would keep her safe from. And yet, he'd known all along he was condemning her to it. And yet she'd fallen a willing victim to Saher's clever hands, to his lips and tongue. He was well versed in the art of love and he was using all his charm and skill to bed her. Heat throbbed inside, pushing out to skin that bloomed with a sheen of perspiration. Her breathing quickened and she lay on her side, her hand slipping down over her stomach, cupping her sex that ached and throbbed. She slid up her gown and circled her quim with her finger. It was wet. She hesitated, knowing it was a sin to do as she did. But when did she ever do what was right? She slid her finger inside a small way and gasped, pressing that part of herself that needed to be touched into the heel of her hand. She shifted rhythmically against it, her eyelids fluttering as she dwelt on the memory of Saher's tongue inside her mouth, his hands slipping around her bottom, his lips on her neck. She plunged more deeply inside of herself and the breath was torn from her as she felt strange tension inside her body, coiling and a sudden release as she spasmed around her finger. She gasped, again and again, pressing her hand against her mouth, while her other hand continued with its ministrations. Then it was over and she rolled onto her back, throwing off the covers until the soft summer breeze could run over her naked legs and breasts. She groaned and imagined Saher there, looking at her, wanting her.

Then he entered the solar but didn't come to her bed. He lay down on the pallet, with his hands behind his head and appeared to fall asleep instantly.

She could have cried. She'd always imagined she was strong but she was as weak as the next woman. She'd have been able to resist if only she could keep her distance. If she'd not known the magic his lips and hands and hard body could create, then she might have been able to continue as she was, separate, alone... safe.

CHAPTER SIX

It was early morning and Rowena would normally have enjoyed the ride through the beech forest. Saher rode beside her and their men behind. It was still in the forest, the only sound being the softened tread of their horses' hooves on the thick carpet of twigs and bracken on the forest floor, and the birdsong and rustling leaves of the majestic beech trees above them. But it was not still in her mind which constantly worried about the fortune hidden in casks in her warehouse. The warehouse was under constant guard—day and night—but it wouldn't be long before suspicions were roused. It had to be moved soon. But it could not be moved while Saher was glued to her side.

"Are you sure you can spare the time to go hawking, sir? Shouldn't you be in Norwich, on business?"

"I will go when I'm ready. I intend to claim the attentions of my wife before I leave here."

"And what do you think I will do if you leave me 'unclaimed'? Raise an army? Bar the door?"

"I'm sure you're capable of all of those things." He leaned over and grabbed the reins of her horse, pulling her towards him until their legs were pressed against each other. "But I know how to bring you to my side. I know we will be good together. I just need to convince you of this matter."

"By seducing me?"

"I can think of no more effective way. And, no way more suiting to my desire."

She yanked the reins back into her hands and urged her horse on, shooting him an arch look. "So... interesting, if I wish you away, I need to sleep with you."

He frowned. "Admit it, you do not wish me away. You enjoy our talk, our touches, our kisses."

She refused to look at him, to give him the satisfaction of knowing he was correct. "I certainly do *not* admit it. But you have given me a quandary. I have no liking for the presence of a husband watching my every move. I have no liking to share my control of the estate and, contrary to what you may think, I have no liking to be bedded. And yet you will not leave me in peace until you have bedded me."

"So, 'tis easily solved. Come, we should return at once to the castle solar. There I can do the task at hand."

Her lips threatened to curve into a smile at the combined look of humour and lust in his eyes. She bit her lip, trying to compose her face into a haughty expression. She feared she did not succeed. "Sir, it would not be proper."

"And you are so proper, my lady." He grinned, smacked her horse on the backside and they both galloped off to where his men were waiting with the hawks.

Rowena followed the course of the tawny-plumed falcon as it soared into the sunshine until the brightness made her eyes water and she had to look away. Saher stood, hands on hips, watching the bird he'd just released enjoy its new-found freedom. But, she realized, he stood with the confidence and knowledge that he might have set him free, but that the bird would return.

They watched him swoop and soar in sheer joy before suddenly plummeting down to earth, then returning to Saher's outstretched hand, with prey in its beak.

"He's young, this one. Smaller than the female." Saher took away the prey and tossed it into a bag.

Rowena watched, mesmerized as Saher calmed the young falcon, who was skittish with excitement at the kill, smoothing his ruffled feathers until he positively preened to his touch. Then, he slipped on the hood and the bird relaxed under its comfort.

"Try this one." Saher beckoned to a squire who presented Rowena with a female falcon, much larger than the male, who lifted her head proudly once the hood had been removed and looked around serenely, as if it not much mattered whether she was hooded or not.

"She is beautiful."

"And she knows it. Is she too heavy?"

She was heavy but Rowena would never admit it. She lifted her higher, straining her muscles. "No, I can manage. I'm used to doing more than embroidering pretty pictures."

Saher reached over and ran his fingers along the long muscle of her arm. She closed her eyes briefly as if she, too, were the female falcon, responding to her master's touch. Then she turned away and let loose the bird. This bird rose higher than the male, and did not swoop with delight but flew with a focus and surety which entranced Rowena.

"Your birds are well trained, sir."

His eyes searched her face with an insolent expression. "I make sure of it."

She turned away suddenly, torn by her arousal and fearful at what his words implied.

The hours slipped by, judging by the lowering of the sun in the sky and the sacks full of rabbits and other small prey that would supplement the castle's kitchen.

The last bird returned to the gloved hand of the man they knew instinctively to be their master—Saher, who now held Rowena's full attention. His strength, control and command of the birds had impressed Rowena, despite herself and now that the shadows were lengthening she allowed herself to admire him—his long dark hair pushed away from a face of chiseled cheekbones and strong lines. She watched in a daze, feeling as languid as the hot afternoon, as he quieted the bird. He whispered words that made the bird shiver and sink into his feathers before passing him to one of his men.

She should speak, she should mount her horse and return to the castle. But she did neither of these things. Instead, the daze lingered and her eyes dropped to his lips when he turned to her. She turned away immediately but not before he'd smiled a private smile that created a low, fluttering tension deep within. She walked over to her horse and fiddled with the reins as she remembered how his hard cock had pressed against her belly the previous night, imagining it in place of her fingers, seeking out her damp heat. Hot colour flushed her cheeks.

What was she waiting for? If she truly wanted him gone—at least for a while—then she knew how to effect it.

"Are you ready to return, my lady?" She jumped around startled, not realizing he was so close.

She opened her mouth to speak but it felt parched, dry. She licked her lips and swallowed, her eyes seeking his mouth once more, which was now curled into a sensuous smile. "Dismiss the servants."

CHAPTER SEVEN

He cocked his head to one side in surprise and then shouted a few words at the men who promptly took the birds and left the clearing. They were quite alone.

"And what, lady, do you have in mind?"

"Something that may as well be done in the fields, with the animals, among the flowers." She looked around. There was not a soul to be seen. The clearing in the woods glowed in the late summer sunshine, its grasses interspersed with the wildflowers—from the yellow of Mary's Bedstraw, to the vivid blue of the Mary's Slipper. She sighed and sat amongst the flowers. "It's beautiful here."

He sat beside her and plucked some of the pale yellow flowers and brought them up to her face. He gently pushed away her hood and one by one joined them together until they wove through her hair. "Summer... a time for lovers. It's ever been that way."

Gone was the stranger who wanted to rob her of her inheritance. In his place was a man whose dark eyes were hot with desire. She reached out to touch his cheek with tentative fingers and he caught her hand with his, turning it against his lips and kissing the palm of her hand.

Her heart beat till she thought it would pound out of her chest. His lips against her palm felt daring and intimate, yet it didn't warn her off, merely made her want more. She rose on her knees to him and brought her face to his. He smiled, knowing what she wanted and closed the distance by slipping his hand behind her head and bringing her to him.

Any lingering thought of resistance, of her plan to make him leave, of the morrow, vanished under the passion his lips incited. As the kiss deepened—their mouths opening and their tongues tangling—her body was shot through with a need so urgent she could hardly breathe. He thrust his fingers through her hair, loosening it, tossing her hood to the sweet-scented ground. His lips moved down from her mouth, and, breathless, she arched back, exposing her throat to his mouth and her chest to his lips.

He thrust down her gown, exposing her full white breasts, their cherry red tips tight as buds. His smile was short-lived as he moved his mouth first to one nipple—flicked it with his tongue and then sucked hard—and then the other. She gasped at the exquisite pleasure that consumed her and closed her eyes, her breathing coming fast as her body became overwhelmed with sensation.

He pulled away and stroked her face. "You are beautiful, my lady." He put his arms around her and they rolled to the ground as one, the scented grasses crushing beneath their bodies as they lay on their sides. He kissed her and she surrendered to the mindless bliss of sensation that his lips, his tongue and his hands created in every part of her body.

Then he moved, eased himself away from her and his head blocked out the sun, casting her into shadow, revealing the tower on the hill that dominated everything. At the same moment she felt his rigid cock straining at his hose, against her.

She froze.

He pulled away. "What is the matter? You look as if you've seen a ghost."

She shivered. "I cannot, Saher, I cannot do this." She struggled up to sitting and covered her face with her hands, whether for shame, embarrassment or fear, she couldn't have said.

"And what is it exactly you cannot do? I think your response has proven to both of us that your body is ready for mine, that you can enjoy our coupling more than many. He knelt behind her and gripped her hips, bringing her to lie with her head against his chest. "You want me and you shall have me." He kissed the top of her head but she shook it and stood up, swaying unsteadily.

"No, Saher."

To her chagrin, he simply smiled as if she'd not said a word. "Look at you." He rose and ran his fingers over her nipples, visible through her flower-laced hair that had spilled around her semi-naked body. He laughed. "You look like some ancient dryad, some siren of the land, about to seduce a man, to suck a man dry."

She frowned at his words, recalling her mother's intemperate passions and also her own first lover, who preferred a meeker love to her own. She awkwardly tried to pull on her robe once more, to cover her nakedness. "You see me as some unholy demon of a woman? Someone to be feared?"

It was his turn to frown. "Feared? Why would you think that?" He helped her adjust her clothing for her, tucking in her chemise and gown and smoothing it under her bliaut.

She shrugged. "Because…" Should she admit that her one and only lover had found her passion too overwhelming and had left her because of it?

"Rowena. Tell me, what do you know of sex?"

"I know of sex. I have lain with a man before." She looked up at him with a defensiveness that made him laugh.

"Indeed? I am not shocked, my lady, although no doubt I should be. I guessed as much. For someone as passionate as yourself, there must be a reason you have sworn off men. It's simple. You must have chosen poorly to have been disappointed." He lifted her chin. "I will not disappoint, nor will I leave. Lay down, my lady and listen."

The replies began to form in her head, only to die on her lips. She lay down, curled on her side and watched him sit opposite, idly pick a flower and tickle her hand with it. "So, sir, what tale will you tell me?"

"No tale, my lady, but a description of my intent. First, I would explore your body." He smiled, a slow smile that heated her stomach. She smiled back. "I wouldn't be able to move past your breasts for some time for they are indeed, perfect, and there is much to be admired. With my fingers, with my lips, with my tongue."

She shivered and clenched herself inside but her eyes didn't stray from his. "Go on."

"I'd lave my tongue against that cherry red nipple until it grew tight under my caresses. Then I'd take your breast into my mouth, and suckle until you feel like you're going to explode. You know that feeling, don't you?"

She swallowed and nodded, the blush on her face telling him her answer.

"Then, I would strip you of all your clothes." He shifted himself and she could see he was aroused. For the life of her she could not lift her eyes from the thick rod that pushed against his britches. "Do you know what I would do then?"

She shook her head, unable to speak a word.

"I would take my mouth and lick you. I would like to taste you. I would explore you with my fingers, with my tongue, I would discover where you like to be touched, where you liked to be teased and tasted."

"And I," her voice was faint. "What would I do?"

He smiled. "Not lie quietly, that much I am sure." He took a blade of grass and stroked it up her neck. She grabbed it and drew it into her mouth, sucking the grassy liquid from the blade.

"Then what?"

He gazed distractedly at her lips sucking at the blade of grass, before speaking again.

"Then, you would lay there, the air quickening from your open lips, your quim, wet and ready for me. And you would lie back and open your legs for me."

"What if I did not?"

"I would push them open."

"What if my arms held your arms tight so they could not push them open?"

"Then, I would take the long train of silk from your hood and wrap it around those beautiful wrists and tie them tight so you were held for my pleasure."

"Held? But I would not like to be held." She frowned for a minute but her curiosity won out. She looked up at him and held his gaze with dark, dark aroused eyes. "And then?"

"I would feel your sex, stroke it with my finger, watch you move, watch you wriggle against me, watch you wanting more. Then," he shrugged, "I would know you are ready for me and I would plunge my cock into you and you would receive me. It may feel tight to begin with, but, after? Nicely tight."

"But..." she stayed her hand on his. "Would you not roll me over first?"

"Ah, your knowledge is surely limited. But, yes, I *could* roll you over and take you from behind. Some women like it thus. But I would like to watch you. You have a face that shows exactly what you are thinking. As it does now."

"And what is it I'm thinking now?"

"That your curiosity is vying with your need for control. You want me, but you're scared about the strength of your body's hunger."

She looked away quickly. "Maybe..."

"But there is no need to be scared. You will be too busy enjoying the movement of my cock inside you."

She gulped and clutched him. "Stop, Saher."

"Why? There is nothing to be afraid of, nothing to be scared about. You know it truly. Your body knows it. You're wet now, aren't you?"

She nodded, reluctantly.

"And you will be even wetter, even more ready for me, I'll make sure of that. And... after that, there will be nothing but pleasure."

She drew in a deep, shuddering breath. She knew of what pleasure he spoke. He'd nearly brought her to its height with just a few kisses.

He took her hand. "You must trust me, Rowena. The circumstances of our meeting leaves much to be desired but, for better or for worse we are to be together. And I'm thinking it will be much for the better."

"For whom?"

"For both of us, if you'd let it, if you'd trust me."

She bit her lip, uncertainly. "Trust you? 'Tis a lot to ask."

"Not of a husband, it isn't. And I am yours, whether you desired it or not. You must trust me with yourself, your body, your mind, your future. I would know all about you. I want to know everything about you, I *need* to know the truth of you. There's been enough deceit in my life to recognize it, and to hate it for such."

Deceit. The word that so aptly described what she was about to do, damped down the ardor that his touch had ignited. She looked up at the now sunless sky behind the tower. "The light, 'tis fading. People will be wondering where we are."

He rose, picked up her hood and brought it over her hair, still mussed and sprinkled with grass and flowers. He carefully tucked her hair under her hood. "My wild lady. I might be marrying you, but I still want you wild. I might tie your hands at night when we are alone, but I would not have you tamed for the world."

She smoothed her hair and fixed her hood. "And I would not be tamed, my lord. I cannot be. I would die." She glanced up at the jagged-edged tower that dominated the skyline. "'Tis getting late, sir. We should return."

He followed her gaze to the tower. "What place is that?"

She shrugged. "Nothing. Just an old place."

He looked from the tower, to her, back to the tower again. "A 'nothing' place that makes you shudder and casts fear into your eyes? Tell me about it."

"'Twas a place used for imprisonment."

"Take me there."

"'Tis late, we should return to the castle."

"Not yet. I would have you show me this place."

She bit her lip to try to stem the trembling that just the thought of seeing the tower induced. But she wouldn't give way to fear. "As you wish."

CHAPTER EIGHT

Rowena kept her horse to a walking pace, partly because the forest became more overgrown as they approached the top of the hill, and partly because she had no wish to arrive. Eventually they emerged into a small clearing from which the ruin soared high into the blue sky above them. They dismounted and tethered the horses. "This is it. You see, it's nothing much."

"Then why does that look come into your eyes?" He narrowed his own, consideringly. "Like a veil of fear." She shrugged but turned away, not wanting to give herself away further. "Come, I wish you to show it me." They walked over and looked inside. "An unwelcoming place. 'Tis on Gresham land?"

She nodded. "It was the first castle, so I believe, abandoned. A place where things were left... forgotten about." She tried to turn away but he brought her head round to face him.

"Tell me."

And just with that touch of his hand under her chin, she felt the fear melt a little. She looked up into eyes that were interested and kind. "It was my mother... She... was not my father's equal in temperament. There was madness on her side of the family, and her behaviour had become increasingly strange. She sought refuge in the arms of other men and ceased to hide it. I heard rumours growing up, none of which I fully understood until the night when Melisende was born. You see Melisende looks nothing like either me or Angelique. I witnessed the accusations and arguments and watched my mother leave. We never saw her again. She was banished..."

He followed her gaze to the ivy that crept up the flint exterior, its suckers invading the decaying mortar. "To here."

"Yes. To here. My father imprisoned her. We did not see her again. Not many years passed before she died. My maid says they were not unhappy years for her, and so I like to believe that. My mother was unbalanced, driven by her passion and in the tower she was controlled and lived in relative peace for the few years she had left to her."

"Your father was a hard, unforgiving man."

She nodded. "Yes. But she wasn't well and he had to do something. I suppose he was concerned about her influence on us." She shrugged. "I don't know. All I know is that, for me, the spectre of madness and passion is all rolled into one and embodied in my mother... in the tower. I used to think..."

"What?" He slipped his hand around her shoulder and caressed her, encouraging her to speak.

"That her fate was the fate of a wife and mother. She lost the respect of my father, her health suffered, and she was hidden, forgotten..." She shivered.

"You have nothing to fear on any of those accounts with me, my lady. My mother taught me well to respect strong women. And I do. I am ruthless with men, but respectful of women. 'Tis my weakness."

She looked up to his dark grey eyes that were softer toward her now than before. "'Tis no weakness to respect women, sir."

"No." He brushed a cobweb from her cloak. "I do not think so either." His eyes bore into hers, making her heart beat more quickly and her stomach flutter with desire. "Especially strong women who deserve all the respect they can get." Their gaze once more collided, setting her senses into confusion.

For a long moment she'd forgotten why she was there, forgotten everything except the fire that dwelt in his eyes, heating and caressing her until the flutters grew in her belly... and lower.

He smiled as if aware of her changed response to him. "Come, let's leave this dismal place and return to the castle. I would like to see those beautiful lips curve into a smile more often." He lifted his finger, and gently dragged it against her lower lip. She swallowed down a strange mix of fear and something she'd never felt before, a strumming of excitement that refused to be subdued. "You've beautiful lips, my lady."

She shook her head and his fingers moved against them, this time pushing over her top lip. He traced the edge of her lips, she was embarrassed by their fullness.

"Nay." Her voice was strangely hoarse. She swallowed, desperate to try to be rid of the tension that suddenly existed between them. "They are too full."

He frowned. "How can plump lips, so luscious and inviting, be 'too' anything? My only criticism is that there is a smudge of something..." He licked his finger and ran it over her lips. She flinched as if struck. But it was not the force that struck her but something quite different. It was as if his finger held sway over her whole body from the fluttering of her stomach, like so many moths around a flame, to the beat of her heart that raced, although she made no movement.

She watched, fascinated, compelled, unable to move, as he brought the finger that had swept her lips, up to his. He opened his mouth and tasted it. She took a sharp intake of breath.

"Um," he murmured. He looked up through lowered lids at her and his eyes were darker than before. She could not, for the life of her, look away. "It tastes…"

"Of wine?" She swallowed, determined to try to keep her wits about her. "Mayhap I was over-hasty when I drank after hawking."

"No, it's of the grass you sucked. But it tastes more than grass now. Something like cinnamon, apples and heather. Not sweet, not sour, but spicy, delicious."

"I know not what you mean."

"It tastes of you, Rowena."

She gasped as his head dipped down to hers but there was no kiss. "Come, my lady, I will take you away from such sorrowful memories."

Somehow her mind had drifted into a sensory haze once more and her usually strong limbs felt weak. He must have sensed it because, before she knew what he was doing, he'd lifted her onto her horse and they'd begun the descent to Gresham castle, away from the spectre of the decaying tower and its constant reminder of her need for independence.

There was no need now, to fret about how she would be free of Saher to get her silver to safety. There was no need to try to rid her body of the lazy torpor of arousal. His words and understanding had soothed her fears. And now both of her needs could be satisfied in the one act. Seduction. Tonight.

The Hall was less festive that night. There was a sense of expectation in the air. Saher's knights had made themselves at home and her ladies and others of the household had become accustomed to their presence. The minstrels played an ancient air, languid and sensual. It was fitting. Tonight was the night she would sleep with Saher. Because he had to be gone by the morrow. And, if there were to be another chaste night, he would not leave and her schemes would be discovered. She could not risk the King being informed of her illegal gains, and she did not relish Saher discovering her deceit. She *had* to have him—she *wanted* to have him.

"You look pensive, lady."

He inclined his head into her line of vision and plucked a piece of the most tender lamb from the trencher and offered it to her. The aroma of roasted meat and spices would have made her mouth water alone, if it weren't for the look in his eyes—dark, passionate, full of humor and kindness. So many things, all at the same time.

She opened her mouth and he touched her lips with the meat, teasing her a few times before she opened her mouth further and he laid it on her tongue. She closed her lips around it and looked up into eyes that had darkened with desire. Gone was her initial apprehension. Within a few short days she'd gained the measure of the man. They were drawn to each other—body to body—and she did not look upon coupling with displeasure. But 'twas not easy to dismiss a lifetime's apprehension so quickly.

"So, tell me, why the lack of talk, why the lack of eating. You sit there like a nun, your hands folded on your lap, your eyes far away. What is it you're dwelling on?"

How could she begin to voice her fears, her doubts, her longing? She shook her head as she chewed the meat slowly. "I am thinking of my sisters. My sister Melisende could always sense when a change was coming."

"And you think there is a change on its way now?"

She nodded.

"Tell me about your younger sister. Where is she?"

"Melisende is within the convent attached to Blakesthorpe Priory. I cannot contact her. She's preparing to be a novice."

"And your other sister, Angelique, the one with the husband you suspect of being cruel?"

"She is away at present at one of her husband's manors. She is kept a virtual prisoner."

"I can release her for you if you'd like me to?"

For a moment a surge of hope shot up, only to be slammed down. "She's about to have a baby and is hoping this will make things right between them."

"So your sisters' lives will be unchanging for the forseeable future. Is it yours where you sense a change?"

She looked at him levelly. "Of course. I am married now and, if you have your way, will soon be bedded."

"*My* way? Come, do not tell me that you do not wish it also?"

How could she deny it? She not only wanted the feelings that he engendered within her, but she needed to be bedded so he would leave her for a few days. "Yes. I do."

"Tonight, then, my lady?"

She bit her lip, turned away and nodded. She'd thought she'd be transferring the power to this man when he'd arrived only days before. She couldn't have had any idea as to how she'd feel now. Empowered, able to hold this man at bay, able to draw him in when she wanted to. He wanted her. And he would have her tonight because she had no choice—not for the demands of her body, but because she needed to take the silver to Blakesmere Priory for safekeeping as soon as possible. With each passing day the danger that her silver would be discovered, heightened. She could not delay.

His hand slid across her thigh. No-one could see. And immediately her body reacted, a low throbbing where she wanted him. She turned to him slowly, gripping his hand. One more nod was all it took and he rose.

Everyone turned around and watched as she rose. There were a few quiet cheers and murmurs of approval. Such a small thing she thought, as she walked with him, hand in hand, through the crowded hall to his bed chamber. But it signalled to everyone that their future was together. The massive candles flickered through the great hall and the fire roared. Everything was as it always had been but now everyone knew they were sealing their betrothal vows. She was married in their eyes and her future was forever changed.

She stepped into the stairwell and he closed the door and drew her to him in a deep kiss. All thought of the people on the other side of the wall vanished under the power of his kiss. Breathless they pulled apart and he took her hand and they ran up the stairs and into the solar.

CHAPTER NINE

Saher opened the solar door and Rowena paused. The candles had already been lit and the bed lay ready. She pulled her hand away from his and walked to the window. There was no light from the moon or stars. The trees and pastures lay clothed and unrevealed. She shivered under the chill of the night air and pulled the wooden shutters closed.

"Cold?" His hands swept up her arms and enclosed her. She shut her eyes as she felt the shivers subside, giving way to a liquid heat inside. She leaned back against his hard body, breathing him in. She felt his groan travel through her skin, sending tingling sensations to the tips of her fingers and toes, heightening her own arousal. His hands slid from her arms, to her waist, and spanned her flat stomach before moving up to cup her breasts that felt heavy with need, desperate for the wet heat of his mouth over them.

Impelled by the desires of her body, she slid her hands down the front of his thighs, which tensed under her searching fingers. She shifted them further up his legs and felt his sharp intake of breath as her palms cupped around his hard shaft. She drew back, alarmed both by her own audacity and his response. But he turned her in his arms and kissed her until her fears were submerged under the onslaught of sensation that his tongue set in train all over her body.

He drove his hand into her hair and held her face against his as first his lips gently moved, caressed and open her mouth. She'd never been kissed like this before. Stolen kisses at parties, maybe, and then with the boy she'd thought she'd loved years before, but not in such a passionate way, not in such a way as if he were sensing every movement and taste of her own, savouring it as if it were the most exquisite food—a food he needed and would not be without. A food he was hungry for.

The thought cast away the last remaining shreds of fear and she slid her hand around his neck, intensifying the kiss, building that coiling and broiling flutter of sensations that charged throughout her body. She felt the wet heat of her desire, throbbing between her legs.

"You are beautiful, my lady." His hand caressed her skin, the curve of her waist and the plump contours of her bottom. His other hand joined it in its exploration and they tucked under her and pulled her up to rub against his hard erection.

She shook her head. "Do not flatter me, sir. I am here, with you now. We both know I am not beautiful."

"Oh, Rowena," he breathed as he kissed her lips, the tip of her nose and each of her closed eye lids. "Do not bother denying it. Because I will surely not bother defending such an obvious thing. You *are* beautiful, whether you gainsay it or not. And do you not feel how ready I am for you, how my body needs you? I wanted you from that first moment I saw you."

She bit her lip, searching his eyes and saw nothing but the same honest gaze that had struck her when she'd first seen him. For all his strength and command, his honesty and integrity never left him. Perhaps she *was* beautiful to his eyes.

He pulled her tight against him and she felt his hard cock rub against that sensitive part of her that needed the contact, over and over again. Her breathing became ragged and she gasped against his lips.

He pulled away and for one moment she thought he was going to leave. But he deftly untied the laces of her dress and pulled it off. She was left only in her under-dress. He slid it from her shoulders, somehow sensing that she didn't want to be totally naked in front of him. Then he kissed her again and she whimpered against his lips. He gripped her bottom, as if the small noise that she'd uttered had acted as a sign, and lifted her at the same time as he sat down. She found herself astride his lap, her sex pressed against his arousal.

She angled her breasts, heavy and aching with need, so that his mouth could give her the pleasure she sought. Greedily, he suckled her, while at the same time, his hands smoothed over the soft flesh of her bottom. She jerked in his arms as his fingers found the place where she most needed to be touched. She moaned louder as his teeth nipped her breast and sucked further her nipple into his mouth. She sank into his lap harder, and the sudden contact with his long hard shaft that was barely contained by his hose, sent her over the edge and she cried out as her body exploded, her mind numbed and a weightless sensation entered her limbs. She fell against him, panting, in awe of the strength of the feeling—a feeling she was used to but had never managed to produce by herself on such a scale.

Laughing, he kissed the side of her face as she slumped against him, her hands beginning to caress his body, just as he'd caressed hers.

"I'd imagined, well, my lady Rowena. You were made for loving. Strong, passionate, honest, you are everything I could want in a woman."

His words filled her with a low spreading warmth that was both sex and something more. She'd never thought that anyone would say such things to her. Tears sprang to her eyes, tears that had been held back by her practical nature that had thoroughly ignored the part of her that needed love.

"Saher, I… never thought…"

"Hush, don't speak." He kissed away her tears, and set her to her feet and withdrew her robe from over her head. Suddenly she felt unsure. She'd never been naked before a man. What if, after all his hot pursuit, Saher didn't like what he saw? Where would that leave her?

He must have sensed her hesitation because he lifted her chin with his finger and kissed her lips.

She felt a deep gratitude which took her by surprise. She hadn't known what she was missing from a man's touch and would never have known if it hadn't been for him. Because she knew, deep down, that this feeling wouldn't have been the same with anyone else. She might not need to speak, but she could act.

She pushed her hands down his hose and caressed the length of his erection. It shifted beneath her hands and she pulled down his hose. She stepped back, suddenly doubtful as to how she could take such a size inside of her.

"What is the matter my lady?"

"How will that ever fit inside me?"

He grinned. "Do not worry, I will take my time and you will enjoy how I fill you." He kissed her again. "I promise."

He picked her up in his arms and took her to the bed. The light from four sconces cast a steady rosy hue over the bed, transforming it from a place of sleep to a magical place of pleasure.

She lay back on it, watching him strip off the last of his clothes, feeling like a wanton. She tried to touch him, but he was having none of it.

"Do that," he growled, "and I'll take you any way I can." He stroked her arms, pressing them up above her head. "No, we'll do this my way, we'll do this slowly, as I'd described to you earlier." A slow smile lit his face as he reached over for the strip of silk she used to bind her hair. Swiftly he tied her wrists together, tethering them to the bed posts behind.

"You think that will stop me? I can easily wriggle my hands from these loose bindings."

"No. It won't stop you. 'Tis nothing but a reminder for you not to tease me. I never want to restrain you. Not totally, only if it gives you pleasure too." He grinned as he knelt above her and closed his mouth over her breasts as his hands pinned her hips to the soft bed. Any further thought fled from her mind as she succumbed to the devastating delights of pure sensation.

His mouth and tongue played wickedly with her breasts, teasing out the nipple, straining the tension within until it threatened to break. She wanted to reach out to him, to touch the smooth length of his erect cock. It was magnificent and she wanted to explore it. But the tug of the silk bindings around her wrists checked her movement. She smiled as she suddenly understood what he was doing.

But... if she couldn't use her hands, she had the rest of her body. She raised her leg until the inside of her calf gently slid along the length of where she wanted to touch. It was silky smooth. He raised his head from her and growled. "Lady, I won't be going slow if you keep that up." His hands replaced his mouth on her breasts, leaving her hips free from constraint.

A flare of devilment ignited in her. She grinned and lifted her hips, angling them until she could feel the tip of his thick shaft, glistening with a pearl-like drop on its end, connecting with her wet quim. She quivered with anticipation. He closed his eyes, his expression tense with restraint, as she pulled him against her, moving and spreading that pearl drop against her, shifting it until it rubbed against that nub that still held tight and needy. She could feel the shivers of excitement begin to course through her body but before she could do anything further, he growled, lifted her legs and slid his length slowly into her waiting body. She cried out in surprise as she pulled him into her, her hands fisting within their restraints as her body struggled to accustom itself to his size. But he held himself there and kissed her and her body relaxed around the heft and length of him, centring her.

He pulled away from the kiss and their eyes met in the steady amber light of the candles and she saw, for the first time, a tenderness in his eyes that she'd sensed, but never seen before.

Then suddenly he shifted slightly and the exquisite friction inside and against her caused her eyes to open wide and a soft sigh to expel the tension. Slowly he pulled out of her. There was no friction now, only a slick warmth as he pushed back inside. The look of both tension and pleasure combined on his face gave her more confidence, and she shifted slightly and gasped as sensation—pure and vivid—coursed through her body.

She felt the tug of the silk against her skin and she arched her body up toward him. Slowly, with each sign she gave him, each gasp, each wriggle of her hips against his, his rhythm quickened and the sensations increased, tumbling, tightening until she raised her hips in abandon as he tensed, gasped and pumped his seed into the very heart of her. It was all she needed, this thought of the intense intimacy of the act, to allow her body to plunge headlong into the oblivion of bliss, fluttering and pulling around his cock, as if to massage every creamy drop from him.

Carefully he pulled himself out and rolled onto his back, loosening the silk and pulling her into his arms as he went.

They lay silent, one of his hands stroking her hair, the other her breast, as their breathing slowly returned to normal.

"I liked that." She pushed herself up to look at him, unable to prevent a grin. "Is it always like that?"

"Only with me." His grin widened. "But are you not sore?"

"I'm sore." Tentatively she reached down to herself. "And sticky." She touched herself and her legs gave an involuntary jump as her fingers discovered just how sensitive she still was.

She lifted her eyes to see him watching her, touching herself.

"Do you touch yourself there often?"

She bit her lip and nodded.

He lifted his head back and roared with laughter. "You, Lady Rowena, wife of mine, my love, hold surprises. I would watch you touch yourself. See what you do."

"Only..." she rolled back with assumed nonchalance. "Only if I can tie your hands this time."

He reached out for her and drew her on top of him. "You ask too much wench. I will do many things for you, I can see, but I will always be in control, no matter what your demands."

Saher didn't know what made Rowena roll away from him and withdraw her gaze from his, for the first time since they'd entered the chamber.

She stood up and pulled on her robe. "So you will be away tomorrow for Norwich?"

"You wish me gone so soon, my lady?"

She shrugged as she pulled it tight around her and stoked the brazier, releasing a burst of heat. Where was the wanton intimacy of only moments before? He stood up and went to her. He had to know. He turned her and kissed her thoroughly and felt her respond with a heat and growing desire that reassured him. But as soon as he pulled away he saw the veil of distance once more fall over her eyes. He had her physically, but her eyes told him there was a breach between them he had yet to mend.

"'Tis just that you said you had pressing business and..."

"And you wish me away. I wonder why?"

She looked at him sharply but didn't respond.

"What are you hiding from me, Rowena? I've had enough deceit played upon me all my life to not want it in my home. I need honesty. Can you give it to me?"

"I..." She looked away.

He grabbed his clothes. "I think I have my answer." He pulled on his shirt. "Yes, I'll be away. One week. And then I'll return for good."

As he turned to go and he saw once more the distance in her eyes, he knew he wanted more from her. He wanted those eyes to trust him, to believe in him, like no-one else had done before. And he thought he knew the way to do it. Yes, he had work to do on the morrow but it wasn't where she thought it was.

CHAPTER TEN

"Are you well, my lady?" Her maid opened the shutters and sunlight flooded the room. Rowena groaned, feeling the aches in her limbs, and in her muscles, unused to such exercise.

"Of course." She turned and looked Birghiva in the eye. The woman's soft smile brightened and she laughed.

"'Tis good you've already taken to the master's bed."

"Birghiva! Do you know everything that goes on here?"

Birghiva laughed. "Of course. We are all very pleased that he brought you pleasure. Twice!"

Rowena felt the blush rise deeply and cover her chest and face. "Birghiva! You should not listen. You must reprimand the others."

"'Twould have been hard not to hear. Your cries and those of my lord, echoed around the inner castle. Got quite a few of the others at it, I can tell you. Lust is catching."

"That's enough. I do not wish to know."

"'Tis nothing to be ashamed of, my lady. You are married in law and now in fact and that is as it should be. Besides he is a good man."

"And how would you know that?"

"Because you can tell a good man by the reports of their men. And he has good reports, believe me."

Birghiva passed Rowena a cup of ale and Rowena turned over in her mind Birghiva's comments. A good man. And he *had* been a good man to her these past days... and nights. Was she doing the right thing? She'd had great plans for the use of the money on the Gresham estate and would miss it sorely. But she didn't dare risk Saher discovering it and guessing its source. Proof of the smuggling she and her father had undertaken these past five years would lead to certain imprisonment, at the very least, if the King should be told.

"Sir Saher is gone?"

"Aye. He and his men left after sunrise."

"And you have arranged for the horses to be ready for the ride over to Blakesmere Priory? We meet my men with the cart from Cley on the road to the Priory."

"Aye, my lady. As you said, they'll be there within the hour."

"Good." She had to go forward with her plans, but it didn't feel good. A little voice inside her said these were plans she'd made before she knew him, before she'd made love to him.

"Are you sure, my lady?"

She opened her mouth to speak but closed it again as conflicting words battled in her head. What had seemed such a good plan a few days ago had now lost its shine. She nodded. "I must. I don't know Sir Saher. I don't know how he will treat me. Look at my mother. Look at Angelique. Both have suffered at the hands of their husbands. Even my father, whom I loved, found it in himself to banish my mother from us."

"But, my lady." Birghiva gripped her hands in hers. "He believed he was doing that for your own good."

"My mother wanted us and he wouldn't let us near. For all I know she'd recovered. How can I trust a man with my life?" She shook her head. "I can't." The memory of Saher's eyes, so strong, direct and imperative, urging her to trust him after their lovemaking, flashed into her mind. She shook her head, trying to rid herself of the image but failed.

"I can't," she repeated, more to herself than to Birghiva. But, even as she said it, she wondered if she was making a mistake.

"Well," said Birghiva. "Sir Saher won't notice you're gone. It sounds as if he has his own secret plans."

"Really? Are they still secret?"

"No," laughed Birghiva. "He's planning to demolish some buildings and build some more."

Rowena felt cold. It wasn't just herself who'd been keeping secrets. Trust Saher? How could she when he was already working in secret against her. No, she'd continue her plans, she'd hide her silver where he could never discover it and it would be there for her when she needed it.

"Is he now?" She glanced at Birghiva. "We must leave soon. But first I must bathe." Rowena frowned at Birghiva's grin.

"I've the maid heating up the water for your bath, my lady."

Birghiva left the room and Rowena grabbed a robe, and pulled it around her, and walked over to the narrow window that looked out across the gentle wooded and rolling hills, up to the tower.

She'd given her body to the man and she'd enjoyed it. Enjoyed him. But she couldn't forget what men were capable of. If life with this stranger became unbearable, the silver would buy her a future should she need it—a future her mother had never had.

The day was hot and the ride arduous across the land, rich with swaying crops of wheat and barley. The rattle of the cart, heavy with casks of coin, masquerading as barrels of wine, was reassuring. They held enough money to buy a King's ransom... or a woman's freedom.

Rowena didn't let up the fast pace until they reached a river where the horses needed to drink. She sat under the shade of the tree and closed her eyes against the reflections of light on water, her mind drifting back to Saher during the night—his cock driving into her, taking her to heights of pleasure she'd never imagined. And then, afterwards how he'd drawn her into his arms, arms that were thick and muscled and yet held her gently, as if she were someone to be reverenced. She'd never felt reverenced before.

She drew in a long breath, trying to calm her heart that raced at the thought of their lovemaking, and at the secretive, dangerous plan she was now undertaking. A man like Saher who'd sworn loyalty to the King, a man who hated deceit—a man like that would not forgive her actions.

Suddenly she felt a shadow pass over her and shouts from her men. Alarmed, she opened her eyes and looked around. Saher stood watching her, his expression furious. She jumped up and stepped away from him, from his powerful body that cast a darkness over her, away from his glowering eyes and fierce frown.

"Sir Saher! I did not expect—"

"That much, my lady, I know. What I do not know and what I wish you to tell me, is where you are going this fine day."

She shook her head and tried, unsuccessfully, to tamp down her fear. "To... to see my sister and aunt at the Priory."

"Is that so?" He came towards her and she moved back, but her way was blocked by a large oak tree. But he did not approach her. Instead he looked over to the cart, laden with casks. "And you are thoughtfully taking good wine to your family, I see."

"I take them gifts when I go."

"Really? Generous gifts, too, I should imagine." He cast an eye around her heavily armed men. "If your guards are any indication." He walked over and pushed one of the barrels and she heard the rattle of coin. "Enlighten me, lady?"

She shook her head, trying to conjure up some tale that would withstand his scrutiny. But, before she could speak, he'd walked up to her and pressed his finger against her mouth. "Nay. I don't wish to hear your lies." He let his hand drop. "'Tis the coin I heard whisper of at Cley. Silver I'd heard rumour of long before I came here. Your father was suspected of smuggling but it could never be proven." He raised one angry eyebrow. "Until now."

She gasped. "You wouldn't."

"You're right, I wouldn't. I'm less interested in that, than I am its destination. The priory, you say?" He looked away from her, his mouth a grim line of disappointment. "You wished to leave me, then."

There was something other than anger in his voice now. Something that found its way past her fears and defences, and filled her with regret. "No. I wasn't going to leave. But I was making sure I'd be able to in the future, if…"

"If you needed to escape me," he completed. He nodded and turned away, looking out across the tumbling stream to the swaying willows on the far side. "But you lied, Rowena. You didn't need to lie. You see"—he walked up to her but didn't touch her, his eyes roving over her face—"I understand. You should have trusted me."

"Trust you? You came to the castle, a stranger, insisting on taking over my life. Trust you, when I hardly know you?"

He looked around, avoiding her face, taking the measure of her words. Then he sighed. "We were not strangers in bed, in each other's arms, though were we, my lady?"

She bit her lip, trying to stop the swell of emotion from unravelling her thoughts, and shook her head. "What do I know of lovemaking? For all I know, the experience with me was the same as with all your other women." But even as she said it, she knew it to be a lie. The previous night had been more than just two bodies coming together in mutual pleasure. She'd felt it. And she knew *he'd* felt it. But she'd mistrusted those feelings. "Besides, I am not the only person with secrets. You… you have your own plans, so I hear. Secret plans to demolish estate buildings and to rebuild. Plans I know nothing about."

He didn't say anything for long moments, only looked at her in a way that confused her. Then he stepped toward her and she backed up until she couldn't move. The bark of the oak tree dug into her hot back. He didn't come any further, merely extended his hand. "Come. I will show you what it is I've done."

"Already? You didn't waste any time, did you?"

"Not with something so important, I didn't. I didn't go to Norwich this morning, I considered other work to be more important. Come."

He lifted her up onto his horse, leaped up behind, and they galloped off, her men slowly turning the lumbering carts around to follow them.

CHAPTER ELEVEN

It was early evening by the time they reached Gresham land. A flock of birds flew low over the golden fields of wheat and barley. Men who'd been giving the fallow field a second plough, were returning to their homes. They shot curious glances at Rowena and Saher, but Saher didn't halt his progress.

He hadn't spoken to her all the way back, had simply held her firmly in his arms and yet, despite the circumstances, Rowena felt safe, secure. She wondered as to their destination—they'd ridden past the estate cottages, the church, the mill and brewery, places where she'd imagined they'd been heading. She looked up at him but his gaze remained steadily ahead of him.

His chin was roughened with stubble but it could not hide the strength of his face. No softness of line or feature now. She turned away, remembering the admiration she'd seen in his eyes at the port, the respect he'd shown for her when she'd handled the falcon, and the passion and tenderness that had been for her only, when they'd made love. Now all she could see was the veil of strength and control he showed to the rest of the world.

They were nearly home when, instead of continuing along the lane that led down into Gresham valley, they turned right and took the woodland path that led to the ridge. The ancient trees spread their thick canopy overhead and the deep orange glow of the late sun barely penetrated the thickly interlaced branches.

They climbed up through the shady forest, its coolness a relief from the heat that lay heavy over the land. Then they stopped. Without saying a word, he swung her down from the saddle and threw the reins over a tree branch.

He took her hand and pulled her out of the trees, toward the clearing. She knew where they were now. How could he, she thought? How could he take her to this place, the tower that represented so much heartache and fear for her?

She refused to look up at that bleak, decaying building, circled by its remaining habitants of rooks whose ever-present dark halo always sent a shiver of fear through her veins. She refused to accept what he was so obviously forcing on her. The tower that represented the loss of her freedom.

"Look, Rowena."

She did, but not toward the tower. She looked at him and shook her head. "No, I can't."

"Look up." His rough growl of command was louder this time.

Just at that moment a skylark burst into song far above them and she looked. Looked up at... nothing. Gone was the tower, a symbol of hatred and fear for so long. There was nothing but a rubble-strewn hilltop under a wide sky, streaked with the orange-pinks of sunset.

"This was my 'secret' plan, my lady. To rid you of the spectre that so evidently haunted you. I wanted to see the shadow of fear vanish from your eyes. I would banish everything that placed such a shadow in those beautiful brown eyes. The tower and all it meant to you had no place on this land, on this estate, in our lives."

His words sent a thrill through her body and his hand that reached out to hers reignited a connection that she'd recognized from the first moment they'd met.

Together they walked up to where the tower had been, to the stones that had been piled according to their size, ready for re-use elsewhere. There was no trace of the footprint of the tower, of the room, high above the ground floor which had been her mother's solar and the small hall where she'd lived the last years of her life. "It's gone..." she muttered under her breath. "Saher," she shook her head, "I didn't know."

"No. 'Twas something I thought you'd like. 'Twas also something I didn't want here. You see, Rowena, the tower stood for something I am also deeply against."

She frowned. "Tell me."

"I tell few people. I abhor violence done to women. I know the results well. I was raised by a woman whose every move was driven by fear. She'd been raped and I was the result. I adored her and was determined to never be the man my father had been."

"But you were your father's heir?"

"After my mother died, my father claimed me and adopted me. I hated him, but I was prepared to use his connections to get me out of the poverty my mother had lived in. And so I went into the world full of ambition to prove myself and make a life away from my father, with an abhorrence of violence to women. Rowena, I swear by Almighty God that I will never hurt you as your father hurt your mother. I destroyed the tower as testament to that."

The walls of defence she'd built around her heart crumbled under the onslaught of that fierce, honest gaze. Tears pricked her eyes. "Saher... I'm so sorry. I was scared you would take everything that I had and leave me with nothing. I did not know—"

His fingers came up to her mouth and touched it gently, stopping any further words. "And how could you? I am still a stranger to you. I wanted your trust but all I'd done is claim your lands, and then claim your body." His fingers gently swept around the outline of her lips that opened in immediate response. "Now, come, 'tis getting late. We'll return to the castle tonight and then, tomorrow, if you wish, I'll escort you back to the priory to take the silver."

His words came to her through a haze of desire that the trail of his fingers over her skin had ignited. "The silver? You'd allow me still to do this?"

"I bring silver of my own and your estates are prosperous enough without me gaining your own..." He hesitated as he searched for a word, a slow smile resting on his lips. "*Savings*, shall we say?"

She looked at him quickly. "Yes... savings."

"Savings the King should probably not know about, eh?" His smile broadened and she smiled back, shaking her head.

"No. 'Tis best. My aunt will keep the silver safe until... *we* need it."

"Good." He unlooped the horse's reins from the tree and lifted Rowena up onto its back, his hands lingering around her waist. "So tomorrow we will travel, but tonight—"

"Tonight." She reached out her hand and moved it over his chest. "I would show you my gratitude."

The immediate flare of lust in his eyes and its corresponding flare inside herself made her shift in her seat. He jumped up behind her and pulled her bottom until it was tight against his hardening groin. "I like a grateful woman." His whispered words made her shiver with anticipation.

CHAPTER TWELVE

It was still early when they retired to their chamber. The lazy, flickering flames of the brazier illuminated his eyes, hooded with intent. She stood, unmoving as he undressed her. First unlacing her bliaut which clung tight to her body, and then lifting it from her shoulders. She shivered, but not from cold, as he unclasped the silver brooch at the throat of her robe and despatched that in the same way. Now she stood simply in her linen chemise.

His hands swept up her body, pushing up her breasts before grabbing the chemise and lifting it away from her. Then he took her breasts that spilled on to his large hands, and dropped a kiss on top of each one before moving his hands to her bottom, pulling her hard against him, and claiming her mouth with his until she was dizzy with desire.

She whimpered against his mouth, as her hands fumbled with the ties to undo his breeches. He stepped away and pulled his tunic over his head. She took a sharp intake of breath at the sight of his muscled stomach and broad, strong chest. She ran the palms of her hands over his skin, the white scars of warfare, like silver streaks through dark marble. She suddenly felt shy of this warrior of a man and rested her cheek against his chest, listening to the rapid beat of his heart. Then she turned and kissed his chest, sinking lower until her lips touched his stomach and her hands caressed his cock that jerked under her tentative touch. He growled and lifted her in his arms and laid her on the bed. She reached for a cover but before she could reach it he grabbed her hands and stretched them above her and knelt between her legs.

"No cover. I want to see you. You are too beautiful to be covered."

His kisses on her skin sent slivers of sensation slicing through her belly, moistening her quim, making it throb with need. She opened her legs, willing him to give attention to where she wanted him most. But he moved up, suckling each breast as he went, before reaching her face. He kissed her then and her mouth melded to his as exquisite sensations shot through her body. Then he lifted her hips and slid the length of his cock inside her, inch by slow inch, until he filled her completely. Slowly he pulled out until the tip of him quivered against her sensitive skin before pushing fully into her once more. She used her heels against his back to bring him more fully into her.

He rolled her over and she was atop him. His hands reached up for her breasts as she moved up, tentatively at first, and then down, and her eyes closed in bliss. She continued until the rhythm increased and she rode him hard, and harder still, until the coiling of desire exploded inside her and she cried out as she pulsed around him.

He drew her into his arms and then, still joined, side-by-side, he pushed into her. It would not be over so quickly this night, she thought to herself. Nor, she realized with a gasp, did she want it to be. The candlelight flickered gently in the summer breeze that blew in from the unshuttered window, cooling their sweat-slicked bodies that raised and lowered in an age-old dance of sensuality.

She rolled onto her back, while he continued to thrust slowly and rhythmically into her, bringing her to another wave of pleasure. But it did not stop then. He continued as before, holding her, kissing her, as his thrusting slowly increased in tempo. His body and face tensed as he thrust harder now into her, taking her with each thrust to a place she couldn't have imagined. All she could do was hold on tight to him, her fingernails digging into his resistant shoulders, her legs tight around his body as he blasted both of them into a frenzy of cries as he pumped his seed deep inside of her, her body taking all that he could give.

They rolled to the side once more. "You are mine, Rowena." He thrust his fingers in her hair and held her face firmly as he took his fill of her mouth. "Forever. I claim you and I will cherish you."

Claimed. It was a word that a short week ago would have sent terror through her body. *Claimed.* The word sent a slice of lust through her belly and she wriggled against him as he became as hard as he was before. *Claimed.* His eyes met hers in an understanding and appreciation that she knew instinctively would never die.

She was claimed, and she never wanted to be unclaimed.

THE END

Seducing
Book 2—Melisende

CHAPTER ONE

Blakesmere Priory, North Norfolk, England, 1208

Lady Melisende Gresham awoke with a start and sat up straight in the chair, heart pounding and body tense. What had awoken her? She raised the guttering candle but a swift glance around the priory hospital revealed nothing unusual—half a dozen people lay sleeping, including the child she'd been watching over, whose fever had now broken. The only sounds were the snuffles and snores of the patients and the rustling of the trees outside the partly opened shutter.

She must have been dreaming. She released a tightly held breath with a sigh and rose, stretching her body which was stiff from her overnight vigil. She gave her patients one last sweeping glance before she pulled on her cloak and slipped outside.

She hurried through the hospital garden, anxious to join the nuns at prayer. At least she'd awoken before Lauds had finished. She might be able to slip into place without being noticed this time. She didn't need the Abbess to find another reason to deny her taking the vows.

Melisende was about to raise the heavy iron latch that led into the cloisters when she heard the sound again—one single, solid thump of fist against wood. She turned to the priory gate from where the sound came and froze. She looked up at the room above the gate but knew that if the gatekeeper had been sober he'd have answered the summons by now.

She glanced at the chapel where the murmur of prayers continued unabated, and made her decision. Even as she turned away from the chapel and walked towards the gatehouse, Melisende knew she was obeying that headstrong and inquisitive part of herself that the Abbess deplored. Still, she reasoned, everyone was busy and *someone* needed to investigate.

Tentatively, she placed her ear against the gate, straining to hear any sound. But there was only the soft rustle of summer leaves of the beech forest through which the road to the priory ran. Maybe it was a servant boy taking a playful fist to the gate as he passed by on his way to the fields? She began to move away but another thump on the gate made her turn around once more.

She looked for the old gatekeeper but there was still no sign of him. His door was closed fast. He must have found a new source of cheap wine and was sleeping it off. The Abbess would not be pleased. Melisende was about to rouse him anyway when she hesitated and, instead, reached out to the grille and slowly drew back the wooden slide.

She immediately stepped away from the gate, her eyes narrowing as she peered through the iron bars, down the woodland path. But she could see and hear nothing amiss. Perhaps the person had moved on? Mayhap it was a servant after all. But she had to be sure. She moved closer and slowly brought her eye to the grille.

Some distance away, a horse stood under a shadowy tree, trembling and sweating, its reins dangling, its hot breath whiffling in the cool of the morning air. There was no sign of a rider. Suddenly a bloodied hand appeared, and filthy, blood-encrusted fingers gripped the iron bars of the grille and the side of a head appeared, hair loose and bedraggled.

She cried out and leapt away. The stranger turned his gaze—brown and intense—to hers.

"Let me in," he croaked between dry lips. "I need help."

She shook her head. "I cannot, sir! I will ring for someone."

"No!" He closed his eyes and then opened them and she recognized the pain she saw there. She'd seen it often enough in her patients. "Fetch Lady Anne, the Abbess, but no-one else."

Melisende backed away and watched as the stranger's eyes fluttered and closed and he fell to the ground once more.

She turned and ran swiftly towards the priory. Lauds had just finished and she found the Abbess just about to enter her chambers.

The Abbess frowned at her reprovingly. "You missed Lauds, Melisende. It's not the first time. If you truly wish to take the vows you must heed the vow of obedience. 'Tis not enough to—"

"My lady," Melisende interrupted. "Forgive me, but there's a man outside. He wants only you. He asked for you by name."

"A man?" The Abbess's face whitened perceptibly in the dim light. "What is his name?"

"He would not say, my lady. But he is wounded."

"Then take me to him."

Together they hurried back to the gate. One look through the grille and the Abbess nodded to Melisende. With shaking hands and pounding heart, Melisende slid the heavy bar across the gate, raised the latch and pushed the door open.

They both peered cautiously in the dim light. Across the clearing, the horse tore hungrily at the lush grass, stamping the ground with his hoof. But it was a low moan close to their feet that made Melisende and the Abbess start. A man lay, as he'd fallen, shrouded in a dark cloak, groaning in pain. Without a moment's hesitation the Abbess knelt down and examined the stranger's face intently. The man whispered a few words to her and the Abbess lay a hand on his shoulder and nodded. She rose and turned to Melisende.

"Melisende, you must look after this man. He's known to me. We need to get him inside the priory, but he is too heavy for us to carry. See if you can aid him while I go and find someone to help us."

Alone with the stranger, Melisende went and knelt beside him, instinctively reaching out to check the source of the spreading dark red on his tunic. He winced and tilted his head back, grimacing in pain. More gently this time, she opened the torn tunic and spread her fingers beneath it, over the rough hairs of his chest. She sucked in a sharp breath as she inhaled the smell of blood, sweat and something uniquely male, something she could not identify, but which made her heart beat faster.

She swallowed, willing her body under control, and slid her hand over the hard contours of his chest. She'd seen and examined labourers' bodies, people who worked in the fields from morning to night, blacksmiths who wielded heavy hammers at their forge, but none had the strength and power of this man, despite his obvious injury. She moved her hand lower, until her tentative touch found the moist, open wound. His eyes opened and locked onto hers. Distracted by his gaze she looked away, as she tried focus on assessing the extent of the injury.

"A knife wound," she murmured.

He groaned in what she took to be agreement and pain.

"Can you stand?"

"Aye. With help." A faint wisp of a smile travelled across his features.

"Put your arm around my shoulders."

"A slip of a thing like you?" The smile came again and settled this time.

"Come, we are wasting time."

He lifted his arms and she moved under it. He grimaced slightly as he stretched around her and clamped his large hand firmly on her shoulder. She braced herself but she needn't have worried. He rose to his feet, lessening any pressure he would put on her.

She gasped as her face pressed against his bare chest, closing her eyes as she tried to focus on supporting him as best she could. But then he slid his hand around her shoulder and squeezed her arm gently. Whether it was for reassurance or support she could not tell, but the effect was anything but reassuring. Shivers snaked through her skin, awakening and stimulating parts of her body in a way she'd never known before.

"Lean on me," she whispered in a husky tone she didn't recognize.

"Aye, and then we'd both be on our knees," the stranger replied dryly. He whistled to his horse who pricked up his ears and trotted over. The stranger slung one arm over the horse while keeping the other firmly around Melisende's shoulders and slowly they stumbled through the gate and into the yard, just as the Abbess turned the corner.

"The gatekeeper is nowhere to be seen. Come"—she pulled the horse out of the way and took the man's other shoulder—"we'll take him to the monks' dorter. 'Tis empty now the last few have fled to France."

"Should I send for the doctor, my lady?"

The Abbess's eyes were firmly on the stranger who was quieter under the increased pain that walking induced. "No." She turned to Melisende and repeated the word, stronger now. "No. You must tend him yourself. No-one outside the priory must know. I'll have the maid bring you what you need."

Together they stumbled through to the monks' dorter and entered a small room containing only a narrow bed, table and chair. The stranger peeled himself from their support and collapsed onto the bed. He lay unmoving for a moment before he opened pained eyes and looked up to the Abbess.

"I'm sorry, my lady. I couldn't make it to the port."

The Abbess nodded grimly. "Aye. Well, we'll make the best of it." She glanced at Melisende. "Speak to no-one of this. Nurse him well as he must be fit enough to leave as soon as he can." She turned back to the man. "Did anyone follow you?"

The stranger winced and nodded, closing his eyes. "I laid a false trail but they'll work out it. Weeks or days, I know not."

"Then we must make you well in the few days we have." The Abbess turned grimly to Melisende, who'd watched the exchange in bewilderment. Fear gripped her gut. All she knew was that this man had brought danger into their secluded world. "No-one else is to know about this. *No-one.* Do what you must yourself. Make him well. Now"—the Abbess looked from one to the other—"I must leave you. I have business to attend. I'll return later."

"My lady!" Melisende reached out for the Abbess's arm.

The Abbess frowned in puzzlement and stopped. "You are surely not frightened, my fearless Melisende?" The frown broke into a reassuring smile. "Just use your skill, child, to make this man well."

Melisende nodded in agreement and slowly loosened her grip on the Abbess's arm. She was right. She was rarely frightened because she could cope with many things—danger, blood, the unexpected. But this man was something else. This man loosed something within her of which she had no experience, something which she understood at a base level, that would further threaten her dream of taking the veil.

Frightened? Yes, but not for the reasons the Abbess imagined.

CHAPTER TWO

With shaking hands Melisende unwound a cloth and selected a sharp knife. She took a deep breath. She had to take off his clothes to clean his wound. She'd done this kind of thing before and she could do it now. She turned to face him with the intention of avoiding his gaze but failed. Her eyes immediately raised to his, which were focused solely on her, not the knife she was holding, but *her*.

"*Are* you afraid, like the Abbess said?"

His low voice curled around her, deep inside, and tugged in an unfamiliar way. She'd almost forgotten what a male voice sounded like. Since the Pope's Interdict had banned all Christian services and bishops and priests had fled the country, she'd been surrounded only by women. But his voice did things to her that no other man's had. She shook her head, not trusting herself to speak as her stomach was overtaken by a flurry of butterflies.

"You should be." He looked at her with eyes that now held a spark of humour that did nothing to calm her pounding heart.

She drew in a long calming breath and slipped the knife under his shirt. "You forget. I'm the one with the knife." She looked up at him from under her lashes with a steadiness that met his challenge. 'Tis *you* who should be afraid of me."

He grinned and immediate grimaced as a wave of pain swept over him. He closed his eyes in resignation. "Do your worst, fair maid. I've a feeling I'll like it, whatever it is."

"You, sir"—she slid the knife under his tattered shirt and ripped it cleanly up the middle—"cannot be so badly injured if your mind can think of such things."

He grunted whether in amusement or pain, she couldn't tell. "You know little of men." He grimaced and shifted slightly. "A man would have to be dead before he failed to respond to the touch of a beautiful woman."

Melisende licked her lips as she drew the linen away from him, exposing his chest and stomach that rose and fell as rapidly as her own. His skin was naturally dark and his body well muscled. She gently pressed the gash across his chest and fresh blood sprung up from under her fingers and leaked over the dried blood and dirt that was smeared over his stomach and chest.

She rose and poured white wine into a bowl.

"Will I live?" His voice was deep and had a lazy tone that implied he already knew he would.

"I should imagine so," she said, affecting the same light manner. "The wound looks clear of infection... for now."

She plunged a cloth into the wine and squeezed out the excess. She brought both over to the bed and sat on a stool beside the bed.

"Wine? You'd have me suck my wine through a cloth?"

She looked up into eyes that held both amusement and pain. "Be quiet and lie still." She cleaned around the wound and then probed it gently.

He let out a sharp gasp. "Wench! Are you healing me or killing me?"

"Lay still! The wound must be cleaned first." Carefully she sluiced the wine around the wound.

He sucked air between his teeth. "'Tis a singular way of taking wine."

She bit her lip as she saw how deep the wound went. "I'm sorry, I'm trying to be gentle but the wound is deep. It has to be clean."

She started as his hand came atop of hers—it was calloused, bloody and yet felt like as welcoming to her skin as the warming wash of sunlight. "You *are* being gentle."

She looked up into eyes that weren't narrowed now, but warm and interested. The unfamiliar fluttering in her stomach that had begun the moment she'd seen him, intensified. She turned back to the wound. "There is some cloth torn from your shirt inside the cut. I'll have to retrieve it."

"Do what you have to do, my lady. Do not fear that you will cause me pain. 'Tis not physical pain I fear, but the burden of memory."

She opened her mouth to speak but, as she looked into his dark eyes, the colour of roasted chestnuts, the questions slipped from her mind. His eyes held an unutterable sadness.

"Ignore my words," he continued. "They are no more than the ramblings of a man in pain." He turned his head and she saw the sadness leave his eyes, replaced by a narrowed gaze of curiosity. "For there can be no other reason I should tell you such things..." His voice trailed off and his eyes drifted from her eyes to her lips.

Without thinking she licked them and then hurriedly looked back at the cut, forcing herself to focus, willing her hand to stop shaking. He must have felt the tremor, for he gripped her hand more tightly, passing on to her a reassurance that eased her nerves.

Carefully she withdrew a piece of torn cloth from the wound and dropped it into a bowl. "There's no need to fear further pain. The wound looks good. You are weakened from loss of blood. But the wound does not seem to have gone so deep as to oppress your breathing, or the beat of your heart." The smell of fenugreek filled the air as she opened a pot of salve and spread it over the wound. He winced. "'Twill help keep the flesh healthy, help it to heal."

"'Tis the colour of woad. You think I am some pagan to paint my flesh?"

"Mayhap you are." She glanced into his eyes and then looked abruptly down again, shocked by the warmth of interest she saw there. "But, no. 'Tis an ancient remedy used in the East that I've read of. I've used it to good effect before."

"And how does a gentle lady come to be so well acquainted with such learned texts?"

"My father."

"A local lord keeps learned texts. Ah, I'm sure 'tis the same in every Norfolk household."

"My father, sir, was well travelled in his youth and interested in such things. While others in King Richard's army plundered gold and women, they were not my father's priority. He plundered books."

"An educated and saintly man then."

"Educated, but not saintly. They may not have been his priority, but he plundered his share of gold—and, I have no doubt, of women—too."

"You have harsh opinions about your father."

"I saw him for what he was." She wound a strip of cloth with wadding around his chest and he winced. She rested her hand gently on his chest, just above his wound and felt the steady beat of his heart quicken slightly. She frowned and withdrew her hand.

"Why do you frown?"

She would not tell him that she was afraid of his body's response to her, and hers to his. Instead she looked up at him and shrugged. "I was wondering... who did this to you?"

He sighed and rolled his head back on the pillow, looking up at the white-washed ceiling, away from her. "Someone who no longer lives, that much I will tell you."

She pursed her lips at the easy admission of murder. "I'm sorry."

He frowned. "Sorry? I am not. He would have killed me, if I hadn't him."

"Aye, I suppose. 'Tis just that I spend my days trying to heal people, that to see such wanton waste does not sit well with me."

"'Twas not a waste of my energy. He was a murderer and a thief. 'Tis no loss to the world—more men will live because of his death." He tried to sit up.

She put out a hand to stop him. She didn't even touch him and he looked up into her eyes and was still. "Pray, do not move, let your wound heal. I'll give you something to lessen the pain."

She returned to the table, feeling his eyes on her back all the while. A cock crowed loudly nearby and Melisende looked out to the window. It was now light and she could hear people already at work on the priory farm. It was all so familiar and yet she felt everything had changed. She looked down at the mixture she was blending, and wondered if anything would ever be the same again. She poured some hop oil into a small cup.

"You look like a witch, with your bright hair haloed in the light, stirring your strange concoctions." She touched her hair, uncovered by the usual veil. She turned to him and felt again the overwhelming sensation. It was as if someone had whispered in her ear, sending delicious shivers over her skin, erasing all sense, all thoughts. "Are you?"

"What?" She shook her head, trying to focus on his words.

He smiled. "A witch, my lady. A beautiful, gentle witch, about to cast a spell on me."

Her eyes lowered to his lips, curled into the kind of smile that would have made her gladly believe she was a witch. She turned her attention once more to the preparation of the sleeping draught. "No, sir. No witch."

"Then what is that you are stirring?"

"Something to make you relax, help you to sleep."

"Not the belladonna. I will not have that. You are most surely a witch if you plan to use such potions on me."

"Not belladonna. Although I have used it," she couldn't resist adding.

"So... no witch then."

She went and sat beside him, continuing to stir the liquid. "You speak much for one so badly wounded."

He settled back on the pillows. "It takes my mind off the pain." A silence settled between them. "As do you."

She blushed but refused to look him in the eye. "You need to sit up and drink this."

He sniffed suspiciously. "Ale?"

An oil made from hops. 'Twill help you rest, but will not make you sleep unwillingly. Here, lean on me."

She hooked her arm around his shoulder blades, aware of the proximity of his face to her breasts that tightened under his quick glance. "Mayhap I have died," his smile turned into a grin. "And gone to heaven."

She thrust the cup to his lips. "Drink." He drank, both the contents of the cup and her, with his eyes. She felt naked. But, unable to move as he swallowed the liquid, she had to sit on the edge of the bed, her arm around him, their faces close. And, for the first time, her mind and body imagined what it would be like to lie with such a man. To have a body such as his— strong, protective and virile—next to hers, night after night. Lust stabbed low in her belly. He finished the liquid and she eased him back onto the pillows.

"So, if you are not a witch, you are not a nun, what are you, temptress?"

She rose and took the empty bowl to the table. "Simply a novice."

"A novice?" He sighed sleepily. The potion was about to work. He rolled his head to one side and gazed at her. Shivers coursed down her spine, as if his eyes were tracking down her back, following the curve of her shoulders, down to her waist and further. "That would be a waste, indeed."

She gave him a reproving look. "A waste? To devote my life to the Lord? I think not."

"But you are beyond age to be a novice."

"My lady Abbess hasn't yet invited me to take my vows."

He huffed sleepily. "Lady Anne always was a good judge of character."

She gritted her teeth, checked his wound and covered him over. "Not that it's anything to do with you but I will make a good nun."

"It may be as you say, but Lady Anne is very astute. She may know you better than you think."

She bit her lip at the uncertainty and doubt his words inspired. 'Twas what she feared, that she wouldn't be able to live the life she'd always wanted. The only future she could imagine lay within the confines of the priory walls. All her hopes and dreams were here, and they would surely wither and die if faced with the world her sister, Angelique, had—married to a man she did not love.

She shook her head and was about to speak when he turned his head to one side and his eyes closed. His body relaxed as he drifted into sleep.

She sat back in her chair and studied his face. Who was this man, this man who made her aware of her body, whose presence played upon her, like a bow over a violin, like a hand tapping the skin on a drum, the vibrations resonating deep within?

Suddenly the door opened and Melisende jumped up, feeling guilty at her errant thoughts. The Abbess quietly entered the room and nodded approvingly at Melisende.

"The wound?" the Abbess whispered.

"'Tis clean. God willing, it should heal well." She hesitated. "My lady, who is he? From whence does he come?"

The Abbess smiled at Melisende. "Curious as always." She hesitated and sighed. "You must know him as Father Galien, a priest from my mother's country of Poitou."

A priest? She nodded. She couldn't face the Abbess, couldn't allow her to see the shock that her words had evinced within her. She turned away, collected the soiled cloths and walked to the table, struggling to contain the confusion of thoughts and feelings.

The wayward thoughts and desires of her body had been immediately twisted into guilt. What kind of woman was she to have such feelings for a priest? Mayhap the Abbess was right, she wasn't fit to be a nun, for how could she be fit to be a nun when such wicked thoughts filled her at the sight of a man's body?

But then there was the man himself. What kind of priest was he to talk with her in the way he had?

"Inform me when he awakes, Melisende."

"Yes, my lady."

A *priest*?

It was as if a heavy metal shield had slid into place between them, creating a barrier big enough to hide behind, big enough to protect her from the wanton thoughts that would end up enslaving her. He was a threat to her future no longer and she was relieved because of it. She *was*, she told herself firmly as she twisted a cork too firmly into a bottle.

As the door closed behind the Abbess, Melisende turned her gaze to the stranger in the bed and was flooded with doubt once more. *Who was he?* A wounded man, a man who made her skin heat with just one glance, a *priest*? None of it added up.

Who was he *really*? She didn't know but she was going to find out.

CHAPTER THREE

Galien inhaled the smell of lavender and dreamed he was back in the lavender fields of Poitou. He sighed as a sense of peace filled him. He could almost hear his younger sister's laughter as she tried to follow him into the forest, could almost see the beautiful castle of Mirebeau, shining brightly in the sunshine. Then his mind drifted to the day when the blue sky had been full of dark smoke—a heavy grey pall that obscured the sun and signalled an end to his idyllic childhood, an end to all his family, except him. The memory cast a shadow over him like a thunderous raincloud from which it was impossible to escape, and he slowly became aware of the aches and pains of his body as he drifted awake.

He opened his eyes and looked at the white-washed wall on which the shadows of branches flickered over bright sunlight. Seeking to find the light after the dark memory, he turned his head to the unshuttered window. Outside, the fresh green leaves of a beech tree filled his vision. The sky wasn't the brilliant azure of the south, but a clear, paler northern blue— fresh and cleansing. He breathed deep, and could now discern other, more domestic smells of cooking and wood smoke, but it was the scent of lavender that was most pleasing, the scent his mind focussed on.

A wooden chair scraped over bare boards and the last of the mists slipped away. A charge like lightning shot through his body. In one swift movement he rose to his feet, groping for his sword as he stood. But what he saw made him stop immediately. She was a vision. The white veil of a novitiate couldn't hide a lock of blonde hair that peeped from behind the veil. And with no other adornment the blue eyes appeared huge, and more violet in contrast to the flush that filled her face. She was beautiful.

"My lady!"

This slender vision of a woman walked up to him and placed her hands firmly on his shoulders. "Sit down this instant, sir! Do you wish to undo all my hard work?" She pointed to his chest, which was bare and bandaged. Blood had begun to ooze from beneath the dressing.

He pressed his palm against it and looked down, surprised at the lack of pain. "'Tis not so bad as I thought."

"Only because you've had good nursing."

An army would not have halted his advance, a King's command would not, but her fierce gaze made him sit down. "'Twas good of you." Up close he could see just how fine her skin was, flawless, with lightly flushed cheeks. "Thank you."

She gathered a length of bandage from the table and dropped some liquid onto a wad of cloth. Her movements were deft and graceful, a thousand miles from the rough company he'd been keeping these past weeks. It was as if she'd emerged whole, stepped out of his gentle dreams. When he looked upon her, the feeling he'd had when he'd dreamed of his home fell upon him once more. Her presence had the same effect as her medicine, a salve that made him feel whole again.

She returned to his side and gently unravelled the bloody bandage from around his chest. Despite her authoritative tone, he felt her hand tremble a little as she undid his bandage and surveyed the damage. Galien was mesmerized by the soft scrape of her nails over his skin, of the tickle of her white veil as it fell forward and brushed his shoulder. She dabbed at the fresh blood with a wad of wine-soaked cloth.

"'The gum has held. It should not bleed again if you do not move suddenly."

She glanced up at him and he was at once aware of the strange mixture of fragility and strength. It was compelling and hit him full force, making him almost forget why he was there, forget the hatred that burned deep in his heart. Almost. But not quite.

He watched her move away to fetch more bandages, the pale folds of her unfashionably loose tunic making her appear more slender, more vulnerable than he wanted her to be. He couldn't remember the last time he'd felt such respite from a person. He couldn't remember, and he couldn't afford to remember. There was no room in his life for softness, for feeling. Only revenge.

"'Twas a deep knife wound," said the vision. "But clean. Whoever your assailant was, he used a good quality blade. He was no rough outlaw."

He frowned. She was clever as well as beautiful. He shrugged. "Who knows where these outlaws steal their blades from? When they slash at you with a sword 'tis hard to dodge."

"But 'twasn't a long sword, sir. You see"—she fingered the wound—"the knife wound is quite small, but the wound deep. 'Twas a dagger, close up, that did this injury to you."

He narrowed his gaze but said nothing. It seemed anything he did say, would be unpicked by her, his lies detected. Could she see into his very mind?

"And here..." Her gentle yet firm fingers swept over his bruised cheekbone and he closed his eyes without meaning to, relishing the long-forgotten touch of someone who healed, someone who wanted neither money, nor to kill him. "Here, your strong bones held you in good stead. The blow—with a fist I think—would have shattered most men's bones." Helplessly he watched as she picked up his hand, and curled his fingers into a fist, exposing his bruised knuckles. "But from the damage to your skin here, it would appear you gave as good as you got."

How could such softness of hand penetrate his tough, war-hardened skin? Not just touch the skin, but send shivers of sensation skittering through his body, finding a home in his groin that threatened to give away his arousal? He shook his head, trying to clear it of this madness. He withdrew his hand from hers and shifted his body so the parts that threatened to betray him were hidden by the covers. "A fight, like any other."

She raised an eyebrow. "I did not realize priests were so well acquainted with fighting."

He held her gaze. "'Tis strange times we are living in."

"When a priest becomes a fighter, aye. But"—she shrugged—"as you wish. I have no desire to pry."

For someone who had no desire to pry, she'd come close to learning the truth—that he'd fought one of the King's men and killed him, and been seen so doing. He'd jeopardized the mission he'd undertaken for the King of France with an act of revenge and was now a marked man with no alternative before him but to accept the shelter of the Abbess before returning to France. He couldn't let his cover be blown by this young woman. Who knew where the King had spies? "In these days of the Interdict, priests do whatever they have to do to enable both themselves and their faith to survive."

She turned from him and walked back to the bench. "Maybe. But..." She hesitated for so long he wondered if she was going to complete the sentence. Then he saw her shoulders rise as she took a deep breath. "But I think you look most unlike a priest."

"Since the Pope has forbidden religious ceremony in England, many priests prefer a disguise. That way, at least they escape notice of the King."

"A disguise? Um..." She didn't turn around but continued to grind powder in a pestle. "That would only be necessary if you were a priest but I don't think you are, are you?"

There was something in the absolute simplicity of her question, of the aura of truth that surrounded her, that made the first lies that sprang to his lips die away. "I'm many things to many people." He tried to keep his tone light. "What would you have me be to you?"

She turned then and he saw an urgency in her eyes, a frightened desire, that swept away the lightness he'd tried in vain to communicate. "I would have you be a priest, despite what my senses tell me."

He nodded, understanding at once. It was best that he was a priest, for both of them. Sometimes it was safer and easier to have barriers before temptation. The attraction was obviously mutual and could be good for neither of them.

"So... am I to be confined to bed like an invalid?" He smiled, but she did not.

"No. Just be sure to make no sudden movements. You may walk, with care." She turned back to her work bench where she was blending some aromatic concoction with a mortar. In front of her stood a neatly stacked wooden tray of pots. Two books lay open on the bench, one in which she had been writing and the other some kind of learned text.

"'Tis well I'm not. I have work to do." He rose gingerly, checked for bleeding, there was none, and followed her to the bench.

"Work?" she answered with a wry expression he chose to ignore. "Since the Pope's Interdict there has been little work for priests."

"Ah, my lady"—he shrugged—"there are other ways of following God's work besides preaching."

She looked at him sharply. "That is what the Abbess tells me, also." Then she pressed her lips together, as if she felt she'd revealed too much and continued her work.

He stood behind her shoulder. She didn't turn around but he could tell she was aware of his presence. Her hands ceased moving. "And what is your way of doing God's work?" He indicated the open books before her. "Healing people?"

"'Tis what the Abbess believes. She does not believe I should take the vows. Not yet, anyway."

"But you do not agree?"

"The Abbess is a wise woman and I wish to be obedient."

He gave a sweeping glance at the row of medicine bottles, the open book before her, and her hands that worked on a pestle and mortar, grinding seeds into powder. She was a clever woman. He returned his gaze to her profile. The white veil of the novitiate covered all but a few strands of blonde hair and revealed a fine-boned face with red lips of a perfect curve to kiss. Clever and beautiful, and with a mind of her own. The Abbess was indeed wise.

He was so close to her that all he'd have to do would be to stretch out his hand to lightly touch her chin and turn her around to face him. And then… just dip his head to hers to taste those lips.

She turned suddenly and looked at him. Her flush deepened and her gaze fell to his lips. He groaned and felt his body react. He was in dangerous territory. He turned back to the desk. "And here, what is this list of?" He cared not a fig about the list but for her sake he needed to change the direction their minds were taking.

She swallowed and patted her pen as if it were as beloved and familiar as the pestle. "I record our supply of medicines."

He couldn't move even though he knew he should. He looked over her shoulder and was rewarded with her sharp intake of breath. He could smell her better now that he was close, a fragrance of lavender—the one that had penetrated his dreams—coming from her skin, and the pungent powder in the pestle. He pointed to one entry. "Woad? You also dye wool?"

He was rewarded with a huff of amusement and a lessening of tension. "Woad is excellent for healing. I've treated reddened, inflamed wounds that have healed when it has been applied."

He pointed to one of the names listed. "'Tis a Persian name. You learn your skill from unusual sources, my lady. From your father's books, you say?"

"Aye. He was a great collector of treasures. I brought this with me from my home." Her eyes gleamed with excitement as she caressed the cover of the book. And for one long moment he imagined her hand caressing him with the same tenderness. "And I have copied it to help others learn. There is a young woman I'm teaching, Ada…" She broke off suddenly and shrugged. "You do not wish to know all of this."

He reached across to the book and purposely brushed his arm against hers. He was rewarded with a soft gasp. "I do. Tell me, how do you come by woad?"

She shifted her gaze away from him. "Woad is grown in England."

"But not enough to supply the demand from the wool dyers. Even I, a simple… priest, knows that much."

She bit her lip and he frowned. If she could see what he was hiding, then the same was true for her. She was hiding something of her own. She shrugged but it wasn't fluid, it was the awkward movement of someone who made the gesture on purpose to assume a nonchalance that was not felt. "We are close to the port here, there are always merchants happy to sell such things."

"Not if the King's duty is applied. Then, it would be too expensive. Wouldn't it?" It wasn't a firm touch, nor a commanding one, but his finger on her cheek made her turn to him and he was rewarded with her sweet breath upon his cheek and the unmistakable flare of lust in her eyes. "I am not the only one with secrets, it would seem."

She stepped away and nearly unbalanced. "I have to leave. There are other patients beside yourself." She gathered her things and brought them hard against her chest. "You should rest and I will return later."

She swept out the room on a breeze of lavender and herbs and medicines, like a healing balm against his skin. He went to the window and watched her walk hurriedly across the medicinal garden. Sunlight reflected from her white veil and gown, like a beacon of light in his darkness.

He stepped back to the bed, eased himself down and lay staring at the shifting shadows of leaves on the wall. If she was the light, he was the dark—condemned to a life in the shadows where only death and retribution had any meaning. And when light and shadow came together, he felt the shadows were too heavy and would extinguish the light. And he could not do that to her.

CHAPTER FOUR

Three days later...

Melisende could barely see where the path ended and the woods began as she made her way back to the priory from a meeting with some of the villagers. There was no moon and she was thankful for the company of Tom, her childhood friend, who carried her heavy basket. He chatted softly about his new wife and baby, and she was pleased for him, pleased for the happiness she could hear in every syllable he spoke. Yet she knew, deep down, such a family life would not make her happy.

Tom needed only an occasional word of agreement on her part to continue and she soon found her mind had wandered back to the priory—to the mysterious priest who had recovered well these past few days, and to the Abbess. She felt a twinge of guilt about slipping away from the priory without telling the Abbess. It was easy to get away without discovery since they had fewer servants in these uncertain times. But disobedience was still a sin, although she felt it was justified in this case. Because from these meetings, she was able to source medicines to help the sick, which otherwise the priory would never be able to afford. Then her mind slid back to the Priest.

If disobedience was a sin, what would the Abbess call her wanton thoughts of the Priest? She'd never felt like this about any man before. His presence totally consumed her, making her forget everything that was going on around her, except him, the curve of his shoulder, the sudden warmth in his eyes as he caught her gaze. Maybe the Abbess was right in not giving her permission to become a nun. But no other life would give her what she craved and what she found here, at Blakesthorpe—a home where she could heal, learn and teach, could live a life where her mind could be free.

"Good evening, Lady Melisende!" The voice came from beneath the shadowy trees that edged the woodland path.

Tom jumped in front of her, dagger drawn, ready to fight. "Who's there? Show yourself!"

Even before there was a response, Melisende placed her hand on Tom's arm. "Tom! 'Tis someone I know."

Galien emerged from the shadows and walked up to Tom, his form menacing and tall, despite Tom's stocky build. "I came to escort Lady Melisende back to the Abbey after I discovered her missing. I can see I had no need."

Tom looked from Melisende back to Galien. "Mel?"

She tugged Tom's fist, still tight around the dagger.

"All's well. He is a priest from the priory, a friend of the Abbess's."

Slowly Tom relaxed and stood to one side. "Very well sir, if Mel—I mean Lady Melisende—vouches for you, then you must be who you say you are." He turned to Melisende and gave her the basket. "Are you sure you don't want me to take you back to the priory?"

She shook her head. "Nay. Father Galien will escort me there." She smiled a smile that tried to reassure but it was hard when her heart thumped so rapidly, as if to warn her of danger.

"Then I'll bid you goodnight." He bowed and smiled and nodded curtly to Galien, before returning back down the path, shooting suspicious glances over his shoulder as he went.

Galien laughed softly. "You have quite a champion, there."

"Tom is an old friend. I've known him since I could barely walk. He and his family are like family to me. They look out for me."

"I'm pleased to hear it." He extended his arm and, after only a brief hesitation, she slipped her hand through his, closing her eyes briefly as he brought it to the warmth of his body. "Because someone who slips out of the priory at night without telling a soul, needs friends."

She shot him a sharp glance. "How did you know?"

"'Tis my profession to know what's going on."

"As a priest, yes, of course." She made it clear in her tone as to her doubts but he didn't respond. "But I thought a priest would be at prayer at this hour."

There was no hint of a smile on his lips but she detected a glimmer of humour in his eyes. "And I thought a novitiate would also be in the chapel at prayer."

She tried to contain a smile, in vain. "*I*, am not in hiding, sir. My lady Abbess believes you are safer in the confines of the monks' dorter."

"Safer?" His grin was wicked. "From whom? From marauding nuns mayhap?"

"Sir! The nuns are neither marauding nor likely to challenge your safety. I assumed you had other safety concerns."

"I have, my Lady Melisende."

"Well, it does not seem so, now. You have time to linger in the shadows and play servant, escorting me home."

He laughed. "My safety is secondary only to that of my nurse. I am deeply indebted to you for your care. You see how much recovered I am?" He held out his fist and flexed it. "You see? Much better."

Without thinking she reached out and brushed her fingers over his knuckles. "The swelling is down. 'Tis healing well. And your other wounds?"

"They are healing well also. I had the best nurse."

She was glad the dark night hid her blush. "Then you will be leaving soon?"

"Aye. As soon as Lady Anne—the Abbess—can find me safe passage. Come, let me carry the basket."

She gripped the basket tightly and continued walking. "'Tis not heavy, I can manage. Besides we are nearly there."

"As you wish."

They walked in silence up to the priory gate, which the gatekeeper had opened for them, and continued into the garden. She stopped where the path diverted off to her quarters. "Thank you, sir."

He smiled and nodded. "'Twas my pleasure."

"To risk your life in the forest at night?"

He shook his head, his eyes narrowed, never leaving hers. "Nay. I like to solve mysteries and you are a mystery to me."

She shook her head about to deny it when he stepped towards her and she backed away, and caught her unbound hair in a rose briar. "Oh, I…" she tried to pull her head away but it was caught and both her hands tightly gripped the basket.

"Stay still," he said coming towards her. She had no choice. She doubted her body would move even if she commanded it to—and she didn't. His hands reached up and unravelled her hair from around the thorns. He dropped it back into place with a quite unnecessary stroke. Then he looked at her and her breath hitched. He was so close, and the night was so dark, it felt as if they were the only two people in the world. "Melisende. A beautiful name for a beautiful lady."

Her mouth dried. She couldn't move, couldn't think of a word to say. She could only *feel*—the breath of his words on her lips and *see*—the fringe of dark eyelashes shadowing his dark eyes, the gleam of the torchlight on his cheek which illuminated the hard planes of his cheek and jaw, so strong, even to the hardest fist.

Then he did something she'd dreamt he'd do, night and day. He leaned towards her and pressed his lips to hers. And for one long heartbeat, one breath, the world around them faded away, and stopped. There was only their connection, of his lips upon hers.

Then he pulled away. His hand, that was still pressed against her hair, stroked her cheek briefly before he stepped away.

"Go now, Lady Melisende, before I forget myself."

For one long moment Melisende wanted to stay, to feel the pressure of his lips against hers once more, to feel his hands that had stroked her hair, stroke her skin, her neck, to breathe his breath into her mouth. She wanted to taste him once more. She pressed her fingers to her lips, wondering if it was all a dream. Then she stumbled away, pressing the back of her hand to her lips as reality hit her like a powerful blow. "Sir! These are not the actions of a priest!"

"Go," he repeated, ignoring her rebuke. "Before I discover your secrets."

Just the thought of him discovering the secrets of her body, of pleasuring her, of doing the things her unruly mind imagined late at night when she was alone, made her feel giddy. "What secrets could I, a humble novitiate, possibly have?"

He laughed, a low seductive laugh that sent a thrill through her body. He plucked a rose and slid his hands along the stem, as if inspecting it for thorns. "Oh, you have many, some of which a few people already know, to do with your mission this night, and some of which *no* man knows. Not yet. But *I* would know." His eyes grew darker as he stepped away from her. "And you're right, of course."

She stopped walking and turned to face him again. "About what?"

He brought the rose to his face, as if to smell it but looked up suddenly and caught her gaze. "My actions weren't those of a priest. For the very good reason that I am not one." He smiled a smile that shocked her with how it made her feel. He walked up to her and tucked the thornless rose behind her ear. "I am no priest, with no morals of a priest, with no restraints of a priest." He stepped back and his lips twitched into a grin that had only reinforced his words. "Just as you are no nun." He laughed softly, and turned and walked away.

CHAPTER FIVE

The following day, Galien leaned over the thick wall of the tower and looked out across the priory lands, the heart of which was enclosed within flint walls, to its lands of crops, the river, the mill and cluster of cottages. And yet further to where the land flattened out and dissolved into the sea. He was looking out to France, to his country and all he could see was Melisende. From the first moment she'd touched him, she'd left her mark not *on* him, but *inside* him. He rubbed his eyes wearily with the heel of his hand. It could not be. Because his future lay over the horizon in a world far from hers.

"'Tis a fine view from here, is it not?"

He turned around to find the Abbess standing behind him. He hadn't heard her approach and he wondered how long she'd been standing there.

"Aye. But the horizon isn't clear today. 'Tis hazy."

She looked at him astutely. "Your vision is less clear since you've been here, I think."

He smiled. "My father always said you were wise—far too wise to marry him." He paused. "Of course, he never said that to my mother. But when he told me tales of his youth, you would often feature. I think he was in love with you."

It was the Abbess's turn to gaze out at the horizon, as if searching back in time to people and places long gone. "And I, him. But we had different lives to lead. My duty had always been here, at Blakesmere. I had the calling early. 'Tis not for everyone."

"Lady Melisende told me that you do not think it to be her calling."

The Abbess raised her brows in surprise. "I thought I caught a sense of intimacy between you. It seems she trusts you with her concerns."

"I was interested to know about them."

"She's a remarkably talented young woman. She doesn't know it though. She's too tainted by her upbringing. Her father was too harsh on her. This was the only place she felt love, that she felt she belonged."

"And you think she is not suited to being a nun?"

She glanced at him amused. "I didn't say that. She can be whatever she desires. She simply isn't ready yet," the Abbess continued. She turned to him. "And how are your injuries?"

"Much improved, thanks to her care and remedies. I must leave as soon as there is a boat."

"You spoke of your father who is no longer here."

"And the man who was responsible for his death is now dead."

"Then I hope you will move on, forget your thirst for revenge and find peace in your heart. Your hatred is continuing the war that should have ended years ago. I hope, for the sake of your father, that you will seek a more peaceful path on your return."

Something gripped his heart then and he felt the old grief and hatred still there, bound together too tight to disappear. "I do what I must."

She sighed. "And no doubt will continue to do, whatever I say." She paused for a few long moments as she gazed at the horizon. When she looked at him there was sad resignation in her eyes. "I've been unable to find you safe passage to France yet. But a boat is due in next week helmed by a captain I've used before. Go now and rest. Make the most of the small time left to you to gain strength. You'll no doubt be needing it on your return."

He bowed, turned away and paused. "I am forever in your debt, my lady."

He turned as if to go back to the garden, but couldn't face feeling enclosed. Instead he walked around to the rear of the priory just in time to see Melisende disappear through a door in the wall, leaving the safety of the priory behind. Slipping away again. He doubted even Lady Anne would have the ability to hold such a one as Melisende captive for long. His smile gave way to concern. Anyone could be abroad in such troubled times. And where was she going? More secrets. Secrets, this time, he was going to uncover.

The pale gold of the ripe barley gave way to a meadow in which meadowsweet, poppies and cornflowers swayed in the light breeze. Melisende had come here to collect the flowers but it was an excuse, she realized, because she simply needed to escape the inner priory confines on such a perfect summer's day. The sky was tinged the same colour as the lavender that grew tall along the priory walls. All around her was orderly and prosperous and yet inside, her thoughts and feelings waged as if at war.

She sat down, drew her knees to her chin and gazed out across the priory pond, sheltered beneath the towering trees. Was the Abbess right? Did the treacherous needs of her body outweigh the needs of her mind?

"'Tis a beautiful place."

Melisende jumped up to find Galien watching her. "'Tis... Yes," she mumbled.

He walked over to her. "May I join you?"

"Certainly." She watched as he eased himself down. "You are recovering well, I see."

"Excellent nursing." He grinned up at her with a totally disarming, youthful grin that made her forget her confusion.

She grinned back. "You flatter."

"No. I never flatter. I speak the truth. *Always.*" There was something in his manner of speaking, in the way his smile disappeared from his face, and in the intensity in his eyes, that made her catch her breath and still her movements. "Come, sit down beside me," he added.

She shouldn't. She knew she shouldn't. But oh, how much she wanted to. She shook her head. "I came to collect meadowsweet." She indicated the swathe of white flowers all around them. "It grows well here and is useful for many things." She knelt down and began to pick the flowers she'd come to collect. She could feel his eyes upon her.

"You know this place well, for someone who's only been here a year."

"I used to visit often when I was growing up. It was more of a home than my own."

"You were not happy at home?"

She shook her head. "I was always the odd one out. My father had little to do with me. I have two older sisters who were family enough for him."

"'Tis strange indeed that he would ignore such a beautiful and talented daughter. Especially when you shared his interest in learning and medicine."

She shrugged. "My father never knew of my interests. He talked with Rowena about business and he'd talk with Angelique about domestic matters. But me? No." She shook her head. "I'd receive a scowl and a dismissive wave of the hand."

"But why? I'm sorry if I pry, but I do not understand."

"Nor did I, until after his death. It was then that the Abbess told me that he was not my natural father." She shrugged, and pressed her lips together in an effort to seal in the hurt that had risen, unbidden, like a chill ghost from the past. "He was not my father and he could never forgive my mother for her love affair."

"Ah, a cuckolded man is rarely forgiving."

"Particularly when there is no love between him and his wife. Their marriage had been a joining of lands and wealth, and was not blessed by love or respect. So my mother apparently fell in love. Her lover... my real father… disappeared, where or by what means, no-one knows or is saying, and my mother went mad with grief and lived only a few years more."

She felt a light touch of his hand on hers. "I am truly sorry, Melisende. It must have been hard for you."

She shrugged. "I was not cast out. To have done that, my father would have had to admit I was not his true daughter. And I was left a third of his estate. It could have been worse for me. I might have been a cuckoo in a swift's nest, but at least I had a nest."

"But not one to your liking. You prefer Blakesmere. 'Tis hard to leave those feelings behind." He took hold of her hand again, weaving his fingers through hers. "You were a misfit who sought solace within the confines of a priory. No wonder the Abbess refuses you admission to be a novice."

"Indeed. Because I am not good enough."

"No. Because you are here for the wrong reasons." He paused and she took advantage of it to change the subject.

"So what of your childhood?" She rose and dropped a handful of flowers into a basket. "Was it happy?"

He tilted his face up to the dappled sunlight and smiled—a rare happy smile—and her heart melted. She knew at that moment that she loved him, even if she could never have him.

"Aye. A very happy childhood. I had two younger sisters, and a younger brother. My father held a respected position in Poitou and my mother made sure we were raised well. Very happy." He looked back down and across at her. She suddenly realized she hadn't moved, that she was standing staring at him, entranced. "And very short."

"Oh," the soft sound slipped from her lips. "I'm sorry."

"I was seventeen when Prince Arthur of Brittany captured his grandmother, Eleanor of Aquitaine and held her at Mirebeau. My father wasn't happy to be caught up at the centre of such intrigue but he had no choice but to support his liege lord who supported Prince Arthur's claim to the English throne. But Arthur was young and foolish and underestimated the time it would take King John to cover the distance to the castle." Galien looked away again. "John and his men showed no mercy to anyone. My family were slaughtered. Only I escaped. I'd ridden out into the woods that morning to hunt. I knew the forest well, had played in them as a child with my sisters. It was as well for, after the slaughter, the forest became my home until I managed to find my way to the French King."

"The French King? You pledged your allegiance to the French King?"

"Aye. And I volunteered to come to England to spy for him."

She looked up from the flowers in her hands and into his eyes, stunned by his admission. "A spy?"

"Aye. And what, I wonder, does the fair Melisende think of that?"

He was testing her. She could see that despite the lightness of his words, his eyes were deadly serious.

She reached up and touched his cheek. "I do not judge, sir. There is only One who would judge and he can see into people's hearts and I believe you to be most good and true in your heart."

He caught her hand and kissed it. "That is because you are too good to see the bad in people."

She shook her head and tugged her hand free from his. "Oh, no. I see people for what they are. I see *you*, for what you are. For instance, I could tell at once that you were no priest."

He laughed. "Yes, that was never going to be a great disguise. I am far too hot and hasty to be a priest. And priests don't usually go around killing men."

She smoothed her fingers over the velvety petals of the flowers she still held. "The man you killed. Did he…" She couldn't finish the sentence.

"Kill my father? Yes. I don't know who killed the rest of my family. It could have been any of the mercenaries John led into battle. But I do know who killed my father, and he is now dead. That debt has been paid."

"What will you do now?"

"Return. Back to France. And then," he shrugged, "wherever I'm sent. I have no home."

"Nor I." The words tumbled out before she could stop them.

He frowned. "But you have this place. 'Tis very beautiful here, your work is valued at the priory. And Lady Anne—the Abbess—loves you like you were her daughter, I can see that."

"'Tis the closest thing I have to a home. But…" She shook her head, unwilling to voice the feelings that had been growing within her the past few days.

"But?"

"I am a misfit here, also." She pursed her lips, trying to stop them from trembling, from giving away the fact that she knew the truth but it scared her to death. She turned around suddenly to find him close.

He took her hand in both of his. "Look at me, Melisende." Reluctantly she looked at him, knowing her true feelings would be betrayed by her eyes. She couldn't hide the truth from him. "Blakesthorpe Priory is but one place. There are many others in the world. Places of knowledge, of beauty, of infinite variety. A home is not made by a place alone. When I return to my old childhood home, it is no longer a home to me because the people have gone. 'Tis the people you love that make it a home. If you have not found your home here, then you should seek it and do not rest until you have found it."

She was silent for a moment as she wondered what his feelings for her were. Were they just the passing kindness of a stranger, or something more? "You will be leaving soon. Will you keep moving until you find your home?"

"I am speaking of you, Melisende, not me. You are young, innocent, with a full life ahead."

"So are you."

He shook his head with such vehemence, that she stepped away. "I'm certainly not innocent and I feel as if I've lived the lifetimes of two men. There is nothing for me ahead that will atone for my sins, no home for me. I do not deserve one. I live my life in the shadows. And *that* is where I belong now." He clasped her hand yet more firmly. "But not you. *Not* you."

They'd shifted closer and she lifted her face to his. He stroked away a strand of hair that had escaped her veil. His eyes didn't stray from hers, searching her eyes as if for an answer. She knew what answer she wanted to give him, whatever the question. She lifted her lips to his.

Suddenly Galien stepped away, letting her hand fall. She frowned until the muffled pounding of running feet through the meadow penetrated her fogged brain and she turned to see a boy, running full tilt towards them, calling out for Galien.

"Over here, lad!" Galien called out.

The boy skidded to a halt in front of them, panting. "The Abbess wants you, Father Galien, and you Lady Melisende."

"What is it?"

The boy shrugged. "Someone has arrived. A man, muddied and travel weary. 'Tis all I know. The Abbess said you must both come to her. At once," he puffed. "She has urgent news."

CHAPTER SIX

Galien took her hand, regardless of propriety, and they ran along the sun-baked path between fields of waving golden barley. Neither spoke. Melisende, because she feared the worst, that Galien's enemies had discovered him.

Within minutes they were inside the Abbess's chamber, awaiting her presence. Melisende stood by the door, watching Galien as he gazed out the window, as if searching for his enemies, his hand placed where his sword should be. A beam of light filtered through the precious glassed window. It created a warmth to his dark hair, a red aura that looked as if it would burn her fingers if she were to follow her desire and rake her fingers through it, tugging at it to make him turn to her.

She took a deep shuddering breath, both in awe of her feelings for this man, and in case her worst fears had been realized. She turned to see the Abbess had quietly entered and had been watching her with her usual piercing gaze.

"Be seated." Melisende sat but Galien paced, obviously ill at ease. The Abbess took her place in the elaborately carved chair facing them. "My messenger says the King's men ransacked a priory yesterday, taking all of its treasures."

"But how can the King justify such robbery?"

"He uses the Interdict as an excuse for his thieving. But that is not the only problem here. As you know, I've taken steps to hide the bulk of our treasure, leaving only enough to allay suspicion. We will be safe from harm. But I believe it's Sir Galien they want and they won't stop until they've found him. They're simply taking the opportunity to ransack the religious houses as they search." She turned to Melisende. "No doubt you have

90

guessed that Sir Galien is not a priest. It was a necessary ruse to try to protect him but the time for secrecy is over. Sir Galien is wanted by the King because he killed the King's great friend and adviser."

Melisende gasped. She knew he'd killed a man but not someone as important as this.

"How close are they?" Galien asked.

"They are not upon as yet."

"Then when?" Galien stopped pacing, but did not sit.

"They will be here soon enough and I have found no means of getting you to France without arousing suspicion. The next safe boat doesn't arrive at Blakeney for another week."

He strode in front of Melisende to face the Abbess, head on. "It does not matter. Even if it arrived this day, I will not leave you, and your priory"—he glanced at Melisende—"and all your people in danger! I will stay and fight. You need protecting."

"Believe me, Sir Galien, we have all the protection we need. There is nothing you can do for us here. In fact we will be treated worse if it's discovered we've been harbouring you. You must leave for all our sakes. But by what means, is the question."

Fear pushed Melisende into speaking. "But surely there must be a boat that can be commandeered?"

"None that I can find."

"But, another priory? Or mayhap one of my sisters will know of a safe place where Sir Galien could hide until the danger is passed."

"We have no time and 'tis too risky to make such public enquiries. I can find no way out of this. All the time Sir Galien is in England, he runs the risk of discovery and being hung as a traitor."

Melisende gasped. Hung! The word clung to her mind, not letting it go. She felt sick as her gaze met Galien's. He seemed to sense her unspoken terror and tried to smile, but the grim reality clung to his lips and didn't reassure her. She swallowed and turned back to the Abbess.

"There is a way." Melisende's voice was calm despite the thunderous beat of her heart. She was about to sacrifice her future for Galien. But there could be no going back now. She cleared her throat. "I know of a way. I can arrange a boat to take Sir Galien to France."

CHAPTER SEVEN

Confronted with two shocked expressions, Melisende drew in a sharp breath and clenched her fists, as if about to engage in battle. For too long she'd kept her secrets from the woman she loved as a mother, and it took every ounce of her courage to face her now and reveal her duplicity.

"There is a ship due at Blakeney Point two evenings hence."

"A ship?" The Abbess's face was filled with confusion. "What know you of ships?"

Melisende could feel the tainted blush of sin rise into her face. "The medicines, the cloth, the things that can no longer be purchased here, that I bring to you…"

"Yes. You get them from Tom in the village." The Abbess looked at Galien to explain. "Tom is part of a group of smugglers to whom the priory is greatly indebted. He and others in the smuggling ring run great risks to obtain the woad, myrrh and other medicines we need from France. And I must admit I have turned a blind eye to them selling surplus woad to market. The money earned has been invaluable to our community." She turned back to Melisende. "So you think Tom will be able to help us find a boat?"

Melisende held her lips firmly to stop them from trembling. "Tom is in my employ. 'Tis an arrangement I continued after I left Gresham Castle. My sister and father have… certain arrangements with merchants regarding exports forbidden by the King to countries he considers to be enemies. I have used the same contacts to import a few necessary medicines… and such," she trailed off, trying not to think of the expensive Gascon wine she also brought to the priory.

The Abbess walked up to Melisende and placed her hands on her shoulders. "It's been *you*, all along? I knew of course that you procured the goods through Tom, but I assumed you knew not of whence they came." She shook her head and uttered a noise that might have been a laugh if it hadn't been controlled so quickly. "I might have known that such an effective smuggling ring would have a fearless and clever leader." She sighed and her frown cast Melisende back into fear. "But, Melisende, you have been disobedient of the laws in the priory. Of *my* laws."

She nodded. "Yes, I'm sorry," she mumbled.

"But"—interjected Galien, stepping between them—"my lady, surely Melisende has also saved lives. There must be some credit in that, to offset her sins?" Melisende glanced at Galien who she could see was trying not to laugh. She struggled to prevent her lips from twisting into an answering smile.

The Abbess looked from one to the other of them and shook her head and sat down wearily in her chair once more. "I hope you understand you are ever further from your wish to become a nun, with this revelation?"

Melisende nodded again. There was nothing she could say in her defence. She'd been knowingly flouting the priory's laws for years, reasoning to herself that it was for the good of the priory. But now she realized with precise clarity that she'd enjoyed it. She'd *enjoyed* the thrill, the adventure, while all the while pretending she was doing it for a higher purpose.

The Abbess glanced at Galien who stood looking at Melisende in unabashed admiration. "Then I think I understand." She rubbed her fingers against her lips thoughtfully. "Is there somewhere where Sir Galien can hide until tomorrow night when the boat arrives? He must leave the priory as soon as possible."

Melisende nodded. "There's an old fishing cottage, far out in the marshes, known only to a few."

The Abbess shook her head, her expression showing both impressed amazement and incredulity. "How do you know of this place?"

"It belongs to Tom's family. We've been forced to use it to hide from the excise men from time to time. It's comfortable enough. They keep it well, for Tom's father is old. There's little there but a pallet and other necessaries. But it'll keep Sir Galien well hidden."

"And you're sure it's safe? That no-one will talk?"

"Very sure. I've known these people since I was a child."

The Abbess shook her head in disbelief. "Melisende, I thought I knew you and yet I knew none of this. How did you come to know such people so well?"

Melisende shrugged. "Growing up, they were my only friends. It was easier that way, mixing with the villagers, rather than risk my father's anger. My father, well, he... *preferred* my absence."

The Abbess's face softened with understanding. "Your father was a hard man." She sighed. "And the people with whom you have to make arrangements. Their secrecy can be vouched for?"

Melisende nodded. "I've known Tom's father for many years. He used to supply my father with wine. And more besides. He can be trusted. We'll be safe there until the ship leaves."

"We?" The Abbess's voice rose in concern. "Melisende, I expect you to return here as soon as you've shown Sir Galien the location of the cottage and landing place of the boat. You cannot stay with him. You must return immediately."

Melisende shook her head vehemently. The thought of what could happen to Galien ignited a passionate determination to make sure he was safe. Nothing else mattered. "I *cannot* do that. The captain knows me, the men know me. If Sir Galien turns up by himself, the boat might not even come ashore. I *have* to be there to vouch for him. They will believe no-one else."

The Abbess's gaze seemed to sear Melisende's skin, searching her eyes for the meaning beyond her words. She readied herself to receive the full blast of disapprobation. Instead, a miracle happened and the Abbess shook her head and huffed, a soft smile of resignation on her lips.

"Melisende, your actions confirm my suspicions. You are too headstrong, too disobedient and too passionate to be a nun. But, despite, that there will always be a home for you here."

Contradictory emotions swept through Melisende. She was a failure and a disappointment to the woman she most loved in the world, but she was thankful that the Abbess had not cut her off completely. Melisende lowered her head. "Thank you, my lady." But beyond those feelings she felt an underlying pulse of excitement filling her veins that would not be denied. She lifted her head with renewed spirit and looked at Galien. She would make him safe.

"Now, go. Do what you must do, go where you need to go. You have my blessing."

"I'll make sure Sir Galien gets on that boat, my lady."

The Abbess sat back and surveyed her levelly. "I know you will." She looked at Galien. "Pray go and ready yourself, Sir Galien. I would have a few words with Melisende."

Galien bowed and left the room.

Melisende watched him leave, her eyes lingering on the closed door, as she imagined how she would feel at his final departure. Suddenly she felt the Abbess's hand on her shoulder and she turned to her.

"Since you were a child, Melisende, you've learned to hide yourself away because it pleased your father not to see you and because you needed someone who believed in you and loved you. And I was that person. And I still am. But I also believe you're doing the same thing now—hiding. And I don't believe it pleases God for you to hide yourself away. You are clever, you have skills and talents that you could serve God outside these walls. My dear, there is no longer any reason to hide."

Melisende shook her head. "'Tis all I know."

"Then, maybe, Melisende, 'tis time to know more? You must gather your courage—of which you have plenty—and do your best for Sir Galien. His life depends on it. You have the courage of your father and the capacity to love like your mother." The Abbess kissed her gently on the forehead and pulled away with a soft, sad smile. "Think on my words."

The Abbess opened the door to reveal Galien waiting, not gone to ready himself after all. "Look after her, Sir Galien." She glanced from Galien to Melisende, and then back to Galien. "Whatever her decision." Melisende frowned, confused as to the Abbess's meaning. "Her courage knows no bounds. Safe journey. Now, you must hasten. And I must make ready the priory."

Galien and Melisende walked quickly away. Once out of sight of the Abbess, Galien stopped and took Melisende's hands in his own. "Are you sure you wish to do this? 'Twill be risky."

Melisende couldn't believe he could question her. Could he not see how much she cared for him? But there was no point telling him so. He would be leaving within days and she would be as she was before. For she would accept the Abbess's offer of returning to the priory. She shook her head. "'Tis not so very much out of the ordinary for me. We bring goods to shore most months. But there is no time to speak. I must collect my things. I'll meet you back here shortly."

Melisende raced through the cloisters, across the perfumed garden to her room where she dressed in her warmest clothes for, while the cottage they were going to was kept in good repair by the old man, it would be equipped only with the bare essentials, and the nights could be cool on the marshes.

From there she ran to the kitchen, stowing as much bread, cheese and pies as she could within the large padded pockets—more used to holding smuggled goods—that lined her cloak and stashed the wine in a bag. But every moment of her preparation her thoughts were focused on the man whose vitality and strength and magnetism could be snuffed out that evening. Any delay on her part could mean Galien would be caught and hanged. The thought sickened but also strengthened her. She would not let it be so. He needed to live, even if it were away from Blakesmere, away from her. Nothing else mattered.

Then she stopped and looked around at the priory that had been her home for so many years and imagined returning there, without Galien. Desolation filled her. She suddenly realized she was more fearful of returning alone, than of running into danger with a wanted man. Was her desire to live at Blakesmere as misplaced as the Abbess suggested?

She locked the kitchen door and stepped out into the deepening twilight. The cloisters and garden were empty, with everyone answering the Abbess's summons.

Despite her fur-lined cloak, Melisende shivered in the crisp night air. She drew in a long steadying breath and scanned cautiously around her as she made her way to the gatehouse. She'd always felt so safe here, a place of security and study, a place where she could be herself. But now she imagined danger lurked in every shadowy corner.

She hastened over to the gate, searching the shadows for him. She couldn't see him until his hand reached out for her. He melted into the darkness, only visible when he moved. Once more she wondered how she could have taken him for a priest. He was a warrior through and through. He knew how to take command over a situation, and he knew how to disappear into the shadows.

He didn't speak, nor did she. They didn't know who might overhear them. Even now, as they stood there, the King's men could be prowling the perimeter of the Abbey walls, searching for weakness.

He touched her shoulder and she lifted her head in response. She reached up for his hand and tugged it, indicating he should follow her. They moved away from the gate, towards the church. But, instead of entering the church, she moved around, outside, to where an old anchorite chapel lay in ruins. She paused, looked around once more, listening for any sound out of place. If the Abbess's informants were correct, the King's men could be here within the hour. But for the moment there was no other sound save the rustling of the leaves in the beech trees in the forest beyond the wall.

He bent down to her and whispered. "Which path do we take? My horse will carry us both."

"No. No horse. We will be detected soon enough crossing the flat land beyond the forest. There is only one way and that is beneath ground. A tunnel."

CHAPTER EIGHT

Melisende could sense his puzzlement as she pushed away the loose clumps of grass to reveal a ring of rusting iron set into a round piece of wood. She gripped the ring and yanked it back, revealing an old well. The smell of damp and rotting vegetation rose up to them. "Come, 'tis but two steps for us, but a very long way to the water. You must take care."

She stepped down inside the well, her feet shifting more securely onto shallow ledges that had been cleared of the slippery moss that covered the brick lining of the well. The ledges were barely visible in the daylight and completely invisible in the late summer twilight. He reached down and gripped her hand in warning. "Here?" he whispered.

She nodded. "But be careful. 'Tis slippery. There are two ledges upon which I stand and then two more. From there, enter the hole over which ivy grows. I'll hold it back for you. After your first step, you must pull the cover back into place."

She let herself down a further step until she reached the hole in the side of the well, covered by ivy. She shifted it and stepped out into a full-height tunnel. She reached through the ivy and held it back, watching, her heart in her mouth, as his feet lowered tentatively, feeling for the ledges. She sensed his relief when he'd found the ledges and brought his other foot down onto it. Then the light disappeared as he replaced the wooden cover.

He took one more step with both feet and she reached out to him, her hand finding his thigh and holding it firmly, so he would know which way to go.

With a grunt and a quick movement he swung himself into the tunnel and landed with a soft thud on the packed damp earth.

She lit a lanthorn and pressed her finger to her lips and they began to walk in silence down the passage. Occasionally they passed under openings that gave way to other entrances to the tunnel. They continued in silence until they'd gone beyond the last entrance.

"Those entrances are rarely used, known only to a few but 'tis safer to make no sound until we're beyond them."

"How much farther is it to the coast?"

"Not far. Unlike the road, 'tis direct."

"And you take this tunnel regularly?"

She smiled, as she tended the light that flared more brightly. "Yes. Tom's father told me of it when he discovered my need. The first time was terrifying."

"Yet you continued."

She lifted the lanthorn as they walked so he could see the long tunnel, lined with wood from which shrouds of cobwebs hung. A rat scuttled away in front of them, disturbed by the light. "Yes, I continued. I had no choice."

"No choice? Why?"

"Medicines. You were correct. The cost is too great for a small priory such as ours. I need what the merchants can smuggle into the country."

"So, while most men smuggle wine and brandy, you smuggle different treasure. No wonder your convent has such a reputation for hospital care. I can understand that the villagers should risk their lives. These are hard times. But you?" He shook his head. "You risk much. Why, I wonder?"

She swallowed, feeling suddenly nervous, as he came close to the truth. "I told you. I have patients who need the medicines."

"But there are other ways, other means, that would not threaten your life."

"Those ways are not as effective. Besides, 'tis something I *feel* I must do." How could she communicate to him the thrill of entering the world on her own terms, where no-one judged her for being less than a nun, for being the youngest daughter of a man who didn't believe she was his own? The thrill of a freedom, of which she only had a taste in her nursing and learning. "Something I *need* to do."

Suddenly she felt the light touch of his hand on her arm, his finger on her lips as he hushed her. He pointed ahead to where a dim light could be seen ahead.

She nodded and they continued in silence until they emerged cautiously onto a rocky promontory that overlooked the marshes. The moon had yet to rise but the starlight gave enough light and Galien extinguished the lanthorn.

Melisende pointed down to where a distant silver line of water could be seen, snaking across the marshes. "Down there. 'Tis not far now."

They scrambled down the bank, careful not to leave traces of their path, and struck out along a rough path of flattened rushes that ran beside the river.

It was a clear night and the only light came from the stars and the last vestiges of daylight that remained on the western skyline. There was no sign of habitation among the high reeds, undulating mud flats and winding creeks. The nearest village was miles away and the nearby castle was uninhabited. But Melisende knew the way. After all, she'd walked the same path many times before.

At a point that appeared unmarked, Melisende stopped, put her hand on Galien's arm, and drew him through the reeds toward an even smaller creek. She fumbled in the darkness and found a rope and drew towards her a corricle, old but well made and maintained. "The next leg is by boat," she whispered.

They settled inside and Galien pushed off, rowing out into the narrow channel where the high reeds almost touched above them. Despite there being no evidence of strangers, Melisende was on edge, acutely aware of the splash and creak of the oars.

Suddenly a marsh hen squawked and they both froze. After a few seconds, Galien continued rowing again, but faster this time. The sound of the sea, beating upon the shingle, grew louder.

"'Tis over there," she whispered. "The cottage lies beyond those trees, on a small island." She pointed to a slight rise in the land hidden by grasses and low-lying trees, twisted by the wind. The marshes stretched out all around them and the coast road was far to the south.

"We'll be safe here. No-one will think to come this far out. The creek is rarely used and fit only for corricles, as 'tis so shallow. In daylight this side of the island cannot be seen from inland."

Galien grabbed one of the overarching tree branches, pulled the corricle ashore and stepped onto the squelching mud. He put his hands around Melisende's waist and lifted her easily out of the boat and set her onto the firmer ground above him. His hands lingered around her but she pulled away and picked up the lanthorn and bag Galien had thrown to drier ground, suddenly aware of quite how alone they were.

Melisende led the way through the shoulder-high rushes to the middle of the small island where a wattle and daub cottage stood, built between two trees, so that it was almost a part of them, invisible until you were upon it. She pushed open a rickety door, crouched and stepped inside. The light from the newly risen moon that streamed in through the open door revealed nothing but a make-shift pallet bed and the remains of a fire.

"We'll be safe here until the boat comes."

"And that is?"

"Tomorrow night."

"Twenty-four hours. 'Tis a long time." He spoke the words slowly as if savouring them.

Melisende blushed at what she guessed to be his thoughts. "If it's food you're concerned with, I brought provisions." She nodded towards the circle of stones within which ashes lay. "'Tis safer if we don't have a fire." She smiled briefly at him and then turned away, suddenly nervous. "'Tis lucky the night is not cold. Besides"—she shrugged, still not facing him— "the food does not have to be cooked."

"'Twas not the food I was thinking about."

"We will not be found, if that's what's worrying you. This cottage looks part of the island. I doubt anyone but Tom's family know of it. 'Tis a place of refuge. We *will* be safe."

"I'm sure we are safe." He didn't take his eyes from Melisende. "But safety, Melisende, is a relative thing. I am safe here, with you, of that I am sure."

"Then what concerns you?"

"You, Melisende." He walked up to her and pulled back her hood. His eyes ranged hungrily around her head as her blonde hair fell around her shoulders, the moon catching its brightness. "How safe are you?"

He didn't move, just let his gaze settle on hers, as if waiting for some reaction, some answer to his question. What did he expect? Retreat? For her to show fear? She did none of those things. Instead she lifted her face to his and held his level gaze with a determined one of her own. "*Safety* is not my concern."

CHAPTER NINE

Melisende's breath caught in her throat as he continued to stare at her with eyes that seemed to devour her.

"Then it should be." His voice was gruff. He shook his head and turned away and walked to the open door.

She inhaled a long breath to steady her nerves. "Are you hungry?"

He stood in the open doorway, silhouetted against the moonlit sky, gripping the side of the door, as if needing its support. He turned to her, his face limned with silver, but his expression unreadable. "No. But we should eat. 'Twas an excellent idea to bring food with you. Come, it's a nice night, let's eat it outside. There looks to be a rough clearing and an abandoned cask for a table."

She followed him outside. There, amongst the clearing in the low brush, under one of the trees, looking out to the marshes and to the invisible sea beyond the sandspit, was the charred remains of another fire, set within a circle of stone, just as it was inside the cottage for wet days.

Galien unclasped his cloak and threw it across the low scrubby grass. "Come, you must be tired. Let's rest, eat and then we'll be ready for the morn."

She sat down and emptied the pockets that lined her cloak.

Galien looked down at the items spread on top of the cask and grinned. "You *are* prepared, my lady."

"We have twenty-four hours." She plucked a couple of cups from her bag and poured some wine. "Other than shell fish, and samphire, there is little to eat out here. But"— she said handing him a cup of wine—"I always bring food with me whatever. Delays happen. Sometimes they are of hours only, other times, I have to return to the priory and repeat the excursion the next night. Either way, the food I bring with me either helps me, or buys me favour with the men and women who wait for the boat alongside me."

"And now it buys favour with me."

She drew out the knife she kept in her belt and cut the slab of cheese and tore off some bread. She passed it to him. "'Tis good goat's cheese. The Abbess makes it herself. She says 'tis from a recipe famous in the part of France she lived when she was young."

She cut some for herself and looked out towards the sea, trying to move her thoughts away from her proximity to him, away from the fact that she could feel the heat of his thigh so close to hers.

He leaned back on his elbows, his hands brushing her arm as he did so and chewed appreciatively. "Aye, the cheese is from home all right."

Melisende turned to look at him. "'Home'? Of course, you are also from Poitou. So your parents, they knew the Abbess well?"

He nodded. "My father, aye. During the years she spent in Poitou with her mother who was from there, she got to know my father. My father wished to marry her but she always had her sights set on being a nun in England. I believe it broke his heart. But they maintained contact after he married my mother."

"I didn't realize. She didn't mention it." She looked at him hurriedly. "Of course there was no reason to. I mean, I knew that she'd gone to live with her mother in the place of her mother's birth, when my grandmother and grandfather became estranged. It was only a few years, I believe, before my grandmother died and my aunt returned to Norfolk."

"A few years, a few months, a few days." He looked at her intently. "It doesn't take long to fall in love."

She held his gaze, crumbling the bread in her fingers as she sought the courage to ask him what she needed to know. "Are you talking from experience?"

"Yes, I am talking from experience." It was like someone had doused a light inside her. She looked back at the charcoal streak of the cloudy, uneven horizon. She didn't reply and he turned to her with a narrowed gaze. "Why do you ask?"

It couldn't matter to her. Her heart, her destiny was different to his. She sighed. A half-truth would have to suffice. It was still the truth, even if it were part only. "You will be gone by this time tomorrow and I shall never see you again. I just wanted to know..." She swallowed. She'd thought she could talk normally, could hold a conversation as if they were nothing but friends, but she found she couldn't rely on the steadiness of her voice. She cleared her throat.

"If I've known love?" He asked quietly.

She nodded. "Are you married?"

"No," he smiled, "I'm not married. And I never have been."

The light inside her flared again, dimmer than before, but present nevertheless. She nodded. "Oh."

"Up until now, I'd no thought of marriage. I had a heart set on avenging the death of my family. I have begun it with the death of my father's killer but 'tis not ended yet. I thought that the memories of my family's death would loosen their hold of my mind. But... they linger still." He pressed his lips together but Melisende saw the pain in his eyes that he could not hide.

She tried to think of things she could say to wipe it away, but part of her knew such pain was etched deep and would always remain. All she could do was make him forget for a while. She reached out and lay her hand gently over his. His gaze rose immediately to hers and the haze of memories receded. Emboldened, she curled her fingers around his and brought their joint hands to her lips and kissed his hand.

"Oh, Melisende, where did you come from? Out of my imagination where hope still lies?"

She shook her head and pressed his hand against her cheek. "I'm real. Feel me."

"Too real." He pulled his hand away. "I cannot touch you, Melisende. I cannot allow myself to be touched by you. Your home is here. This is where you belong, by your own admission. And"—he looked out at the black horizon once more—"I have no home. Nor ever will have. I will be gone on the morrow and you will never see me again."

He stood up and she followed him to where he looked out to the dark line of the horizon, where he would shortly be. She drew in a deep breath, needing to find fuel to say the words she needed to say. "But, I am here, *now*." She wondered if he'd heard, her words were so soft, almost drowned out by the rustling reeds and distant noise of the sea. He was so completely still that she reached out and touched his shoulder.

He turned instantly and brought her to him, wrapping her body tight within his arms. "You *are* here now. That much is true."

She closed her eyes at his intimate embrace, relishing the heat and strength of his body. She felt his lips against her hair and looked up, wanting him to instead kiss her lips. "And I, too, will return to the priory after you leave, to continue my work at the hospital. But mayhap I will cease pestering my aunt, the Abbess, to allow me to be a nun. "That much, your presence has helped me realize. She was correct all along. I am most definitely *not* suited to the role."

He laughed. "You have too many gifts to strike you dumb within the confines and limits of an Abbey. You should marry and go out into the world."

Her heart thumped in her chest. "And who should I marry?"

He shook his head. "I have nothing to offer you Melisende, otherwise I would ask you to be my wife in a heartbeat. I'm returning to France to continue my fight for my lands, to continue to work against the King who destroyed my life. I've killed the man responsible for the slaughter but I have to go on, gain back my lands and make them secure from the King of England. That is no life to share with a woman."

"So… You offer me no life in France, no marriage. And for my part, I would not give up my work. My patients need me, they need the medicines I can source, they need the remedies which the book provides me with."

"But you have your assistant, the young girl, and others you are teaching. And also the copy you've made of the medicinal text. You must take it and make a bigger life than the one you're leading. There is so much you're missing. There is so much for the world to gain by having you in it."

He pressed her more tightly against him, his voice vibrating through her body as he continued. And for one moment Melisende thought he was going to ask her to come with him—marriage or no. She shook her head against his chest.

"You have your life ahead of you, I have mine—both different." He cleared his throat. "There will be no future for us both."

She looked up at him, determined he would understand her meaning. "But we have *here*, *now*. Show me, Galien, what I will be missing. Show me what communion your body can bring to mine." The words had tumbled out and she took a deep breath. "If it's all I am to have of you, then *here*, *now*, *show* me."

CHAPTER TEN

Melisende felt his frustrated groan travel throughout the length of her body.

"You ask too much, Melisende."

"Nay, I ask not enough." He could never know how much she wanted him. Body and soul. Forever. She couldn't tell him because they were two different people with two very different destinies and she would never ask for more than he could give. "But this must be enough... for now."

She took his hand and pulled him inside the cottage. He unclasped his cloak and spread it over the straw pallet. She looked down at the soft lining, exposed and intimate and felt a sudden thrill of fear surge through her body at the thought that she'd soon be feeling the wool's softness against her naked skin.

He must have sensed her hesitation for he lifted her chin so she faced him. "Are you sure, Melisende? For I fear this is madness for you. I would be wrong to take advantage of you."

One look in his eyes made her realize what she felt wasn't fear. How could there be anything to fear from a man whose eyes revealed his desire but who purposefully held himself back, awaiting her command? No, the thrill was in the decision to give herself completely to him. It seemed that, contrary to all that she'd been taught, this man was too honourable to seduce her. She had no alternative—she would have to seduce him.

She stood on tip toe until her mouth was close to his but apart. She was so close she could see every detail of his face, from the stubble on his chin to the dark lashes that fringed his eyes when he looked down at her. "But would it be wrong if I were to take advantage of you?" His lips quirked into a smile and she kissed each side of his mouth before pulling away. "Mayhap *I* should seduce *you*, sir, if you are unwilling to do the job."

"You? And what do you know about seduction?" She continued to hold her face close to his and he licked his lips, his eyes focussed on her mouth, as if he wished it were her lips he was licking.

"Ah, you have me there. I may not have any practical experience but you know how much I like to study."

"Your medicinals."

"Aye. And more... The Art of Love was a book my father found entertaining."

Galien raised one eyebrow in query. "My Melisende, a seductress? I have not thought."

Lust throbbed in her belly and lower, at the possessive note in his voice. "There is no need to think. For I see this is the perfect occasion for me to put my knowledge into practice."

He threw his head back and laughed. "I cannot resist you, Melisende. No matter what my good sense tells me." The smile dropped away and the need was exposed in his darkened eyes. "Do what you will. Seduce me. Where will you begin?"

She closed her eyes as she remembered the sequence she'd learned in De Amore. "I think I've already begun. The first stage consists of arousing hope."

"Indeed, my lady. Among other things, hope is indeed aroused."

"Then the second is in offering kisses." She rose to the balls of her feet so that her lips were closer to his. She slipped her arms upon his shoulders. "I am offering you a kiss, sir."

"Mmm"—he moved his face close to hers, breathing her in—"I accept."

If she had made the first move, she was in no doubt as to who'd made the second. Her offer was immediately taken up by his lips that pressed themselves against hers and took complete control. Her hands gripped his shoulders tighter now. She had no thought for anything other than the caress of his lips against hers, stirring her inside in a way she'd never felt before, enticing her with the promise of more to come.

Her breath hitched and caught in her throat as his tongue traced her lower lip, as if asking for entry. She opened her mouth, giving him the permission he sought and touched his tongue with her own. The sensuous slide of his tongue against hers was shocking in its intimacy. She tried to step away to regain her breath but was halted by his hands pushing through her hair, holding her head steady as his mouth took control of hers. And she submitted to a mindless bliss that swept away all else. It was like opening the gate to a secret garden of joy she hadn't known to exist.

All too soon, he pulled away from her. She didn't want the kiss to end and lifted her face to his, trying to recapture his mouth. He laughed and swept his thumbs over her lips and cheeks. "Cherie, you are so beautiful...

a temptress."

"A temptress." She nodded. "That is good." She looked up to the roof, trying to focus on the words of the game of seduction they'd been playing. "For the third stage of love is the enjoyment of intimate embraces."

"I never thought to so appreciate your learning."

"My learning, sir, gave you a swift recovery."

"Indeed. And I was most appreciative. But this... this is something more powerful still. Tell me what you know of these 'intimate embraces.'"

She took her hands from his shoulders and tentatively slid them around his back, over his shirt and down to where its hem hung loose. She kept her gaze on his as she slipped her hands beneath the shirt. She felt his muscles clench under her fingertips and it made her bold and she watched his reaction as she spread her fingers over his heated skin, exploring it as if she had a claim to it. He sucked in a tremulous breath. "You like this?"

"I will not tell you, I'll show you how much I like it."

His hands echoed her movements and slid down her back, over the length of her hair until his hardened palms pressed against her bottom, pulling her tight against him. She felt weak with desire as she felt his hard cock pressed against her stomach. "Oh..." she sighed.

He pulled her harder against him still, claiming her mouth with his once more, while she pressed her hips against him, moving herself over him, exploring the shape of his body with hers.

He gripped her bottom and pulled her up so that his hard cock was against her sex, moving against that intimate part of her, upon which all her thoughts and senses were focussed. She wanted him closer to her still, she wanted him to fill her.

He too, seemed to have other ideas, as he left her mouth bereft and kissed her cheek, her jaw, her neck and lower... His fingers had already loosened the fastening at her neckline—she hadn't even been aware of it— and he now pressed his lips first to the top of one exposed breast and then the other.

She let her head fall back to allow him greater access, her breasts straining under the suddenly too tight constriction of her bodice. He undid the bodice and it fell open, leaving her breasts exposed.

She was dizzy with need and held on tight to his shoulders as he kissed her breasts and his tongue played with her nipples. She gasped as his mouth tightened around her breast and suckled, sending coils of sensation surging and retreating, before surging higher again. She hadn't been aware she was panting until his lips were upon hers once more.

She was desperate for him. Her hands couldn't get their fill of him and ranged over his body as their kisses intensified, escalating into an urgent need from which there was no retreating.

She pushed the shirt from his shoulders, needing his flesh to be next to hers. He pulled it off and threw it aside. He smiled. "Look at you, my lady, standing there, your breasts exposed, yet your eyes bright and commanding. You don't know what you do to me."

She licked her lips, unable to find any sense of modesty to cover herself. She *loved* the way he looked at her and revelled in his need for her. "In which case, sir," her voice had become impossibly husky to her ears. "Mayhap we should move on to the fourth stage of love."

"I hope it's what I think it is."

She laughed. "Aye, sir. 'Tis not prayer, that's for sure. The fourth stage is the abandonment of the entire person. I want to know intimacy with you. I want to know nothing else at this moment."

His face went suddenly serious. "Are you sure, Melisende?"

She nodded. "I'm more sure of this than anything I've ever done. I want you, Galien. I want you to show me the love between a woman and a man."

In one swift movement he lifted her kirtle and swept his hands up her body, raking the dress upward until he pulled it off her, leaving her standing in her underclothes.

She felt his sudden exhalation of air against her breasts as he dipped his head and kissed them. Then he slid the palm of his hand down her body until it held her at the apex of her legs, his fingers curling around her.

A wave of hot desire swept through her body and settled deep inside, with a melting throb, close to where his fingers were. He must have felt the moisture as he pushed his fingers and the material of her dress that lay between them, nearly inside her. He growled into her ear, a very male satisfied growl. He stepped back suddenly.

He gripped her under-dress and whisked it off her, leaving her totally naked before him. But she didn't have time to be shy for she was too busy watching Galien disrobe. When he tossed his trousers onto the rest of his clothes, he turned and for a moment was silhouetted against the silver light coming through the door. Her muscles, deep inside, clenched at the sight of his cock, rigid and ready for her. She looked up at him with a frown.

He shook his head and drew her to him, whispering in her ear. "Do not fear, my Melisende, we will take things as slow as you desire them."

She kissed his neck and felt his cock pressing into her stomach. She wanted to touch it but wasn't sure if she should. She bit her lip and tentatively reached out and stroked it. She looked up at him and he nodded. It twitched under her touch and he closed his eyes in obvious pleasure. It emboldened her. She let her fingers trail down its length, feeling the texture of it, its rigidity, and the flesh beneath it, which she cupped.

He swallowed and reached out for her.

"Exploration over. I want you to feel me inside you, I want to come inside you, make you mine."

"I *am* yours, Galien."

He kissed her with a gentleness that reassured and, as his tongue slipped into her mouth and found hers, her heart beat like it would burst and all her thoughts and fears disappeared, leaving only need.

His hands tightened their grip around her bottom, and his fingers swept between her legs, moving the length of her wet quim, and slipping inside. She gasped and he pulled away.

With a satisfied grunt, he picked her up and carefully lay her down on his cloak.

She eased back on the springy mattress suddenly aware that she was completely naked before a man. She should feel shame. She *should*. But she didn't. Instead all she could feel was the sheer wanton thrill of the caress of the soft wool against her bare bottom, and the sweep of his hands as they moved up her legs, hips, stomach before resting on her breasts.

"You are so beautiful." He knelt down in front of her so his head was facing the apex of her legs. She felt a blush rise.

She reached down to him and tried to bring him up to her.

"Nay lady. You wanted abandonment of the entire person. And I am your slave, to do as you order." Before she could remonstrate he leaned forward and kissed her quim.

"Galien!" She shifted back slightly on the cloak in surprise.

He gripped her hands in his own and looked up at her. "Stay still, my sweet."

He continued holding her gaze, and her hands, as his tongue lapped that most private part of herself. She gasped and she gripped his hands tightly, caught between a desire to push him away, and to hold him tight against her. She held him there, legs trembling, breathing coming hard.

She could do nothing else. Each time his tongue moved against her most sensitive skin, each time his mouth tasted her, the tensions that coiled inside her ratcheted up another notch, until she could think of nothing else but the exquisite sensations that coursed through her body, intensifying until she felt a burst of release that made her cry out.

Only then did Galien raise himself, a smile on his face and his hands sweep up her stomach and cup her breasts. He eased his body over hers and kissed her breasts, her neck, before settling on her lips.

Despite the release, Melisende soon felt another wave of desire wash through her as his tongue explored her mouth, and his hands her breasts. She wriggled her hips against his, caressing his smooth back and lower, curling her fingers around his bottom, feeling the flex of his muscles as he moved against her.

He pulled his mouth from hers but their bodies continued to move against each other, their breathing coming hard now.

"Melisende... I—"

She brought her finger to his lips. "Hush. There's nothing left to say. I want you." She had no idea where her forward talk came from and did not question it. For it was as natural as breathing, that he should be inside her.

His lips curled into a slow, lascivious smile. "Where?" He touched the place that ached for him and she moaned. "Here?"

She nodded, swallowing hard, fighting for a control that had been lost the minute he'd kissed her. She squirmed against the ministrations of his hand. "Galien! I cannot wait."

"You won't have to wait. Because I want you more than anything else in my life."

"And I want to feel you inside me. I want to know you."

He nudged his cock against her quim and she gasped and tilted her hips to meet his. He guided her legs around him and with one small thrust pushed into her. She tensed at the pain and opened her eyes, suddenly nervous, but he pushed lightly, his fingers playing with that part of her that sent shivers coursing through her body. After she'd relaxed he pushed fully inside her with one, sleek swift movement.

She winced and bit her lip. She closed her eyes, willing the pain away.

He eased up and stroked the hair from her face. "Melisende, I'm sorry. Does it hurt much?"

She opened her eyes. "A little."

He began to pull out but she kept her hands around his body, holding him still. Then he gently slid back and she sighed, feeling every small movement of him inside her, sending shivers of sensation throughout her body. There was no friction now, no pain, just an overwhelming awareness of how he filled her. All thought was suspended as he pushed into her and eased out, slowly, leisurely, watching her—his movements attuned to her own.

With his body and hands and lips he caressed her, warmed her, reassured her, and slowly she grew in confidence and moved her hips to better accommodate him. It was his turn to close his eyes and groan as he eased out once more before pushing back inside her. And in that moment she knew things would never be the same again. He was inside *all* of her—inside her head, her heart and her body. She would always be his.

She cried out his name and his rhythm changed to short, pulsing thrusts and she knew that her body was receiving his seed.

As one, they rolled to their sides, entwined in each other arms, and lay on the soft fur of the cloak, the warm air fanning their hot skin. She spread her fingers over his chest, cupping the muscle, touching his nipple and then kissing it, just as he had hers, as their breathing slowly returned to normal.

Neither spoke for long moments, yet she knew his thoughts. She could tell them from the touch of his fingers against her skin, from the feel of his lips against her hair, and the ragged sigh of his breath against her cheek.

Part of her, when she'd decided to lie with him, had thought this would be the end, complete something begun in the priory and end it, here on the marshes. But as her heart beat slowed she realised that nothing had completed, it had only just begun.

CHAPTER ELEVEN

Galien lay awake all night, cradling Melisende in his arms as he looked up at the rough-thatched roof. He was alert to every shift of her slender limbs, every shiver that traced goose-bumps across her skin, every sigh as he pulled his cloak back over her body and she nestled in his arms once more. He watched the dreams chase across her flickering eyelids and wished he could see them, wished he could save her from the distress of the occasional whimper, wished he could hold her like this, in this place, forever.

But, the moments passed. Just as their breaths mingled and rose into the bracken-thatched roof, the night disappeared in a collection of heartbeats that became one.

As the grey light of dawn slowly exposed the shadowy corners and objects in the room, Galien breathed in the fragrance of her hair, a patch of brilliant blonde gleaming in the dull light. He felt suspended in some unreal place, on the edge of the world. Danger behind him, danger before him, but here, in the early morning light with this woman, he felt more threatened than ever before. His purpose was to avenge his family and Melisende threatened his purpose. When she was close he could think of nothing but the brilliance of her eyes, a blue as warm as the forget-me-nots that covered the woodland floor of his youth, hair as brilliant as moonlight, and a spirit so much bigger than her slight body, a body he couldn't help reaching for.

She sighed and stretched as his touch disturbed her. And in that moment, as she awoke beneath his touch, he knew that the danger had passed because he'd succumbed. The pressure of grief and responsibility to avenge his family had slid away, consumed by the love he felt for the woman in his arms. She taken away his shadows, just as the sun robs the night of its darkness. It suddenly became clear to him what he had to do. He kissed her cheek and brought her closer to him but, before he could speak, she'd rolled toward him, and her naked breasts were pressed against his chest, her lips close to his, her hips against his belly and her thighs... her thighs, soft around his hard cock.

He groaned and she smiled, the most completely sensuous, enticing smile he'd ever seen in a woman. He dipped his head to hers and kissed her. "Good morn, sleepy lady."

"'Tis indeed good. And"—she moved slightly and her thighs moved once more against him—"I'm not so sleepy now." Her lips twisted into a shy smile.

He laughed and brushed his lips against hers, trying to focus on his thoughts, rather than the way her body moved against his. "So I see." And so he could also *feel*, but they needed to talk. The daylight was gaining strength with each passing minute.

But another delicate shift of her hips was enough to break his control. He rolled her over until he was on top of her, his hips pinning her to the bed.

He dipped his head and placed a kiss on each soft breast. She arched her back still further and he needed no further invitation. He took first one, then the other breast into his mouth, using his tongue gently to begin with. But as her breathing shortened, he suckled her nipples harder until they grew taut with need. All thought of doing anything with this woman other than making love, left his mind.

His hands roamed over her body—from her flushed cheeks, her neck, her arms, slender yet strong, and her stomach and lower... She was wet for him and as his fingers gently slid against her, teasing her, she opened her legs.

"Are you sure?" He murmured against her breasts.

In answer, she reached down and took his cock in her hands and slid it against her quim. "I'm sure. I want you inside me, completely," she whispered into his ear, as she slid her legs open wider still, until the head of his cock lay against her.

He pushed slowly inside her, easing into her, knowing she could still be sore, but feeling her so wet that he knew that pleasure would soon overcome any discomfort.

Her hands reached around him, tracing the curves of his muscles before descending to his bottom, which she gripped as if encouraging him to plunge harder into her. He obliged and was rewarded with a gasp, and a flutter of pale eyelids, the long lashes a charcoal crescent against her flushed cheeks. He withdrew slowly and just as her eyes were beginning to open once more, he plunged into her again. She gasped louder and gripped his behind tighter as he slowly withdrew. Again he thrust into her, mesmerized by the sight of her pale face, eyes closed, lips parted.

He rubbed his thumb beneath her full lower lip and she opened her mouth further, as if trying to capture him, just as her body was capturing him, lower down. She flicked her tongue against his thumb and he dipped it into her mouth. Her lips closed around it briefly before she flung her head to one side as the panting gave way to moaning, which gave way to a shout of his name as he continued to thrust deep inside her, revelling in the silky caresses of her quim around his shaft.

It was only when she opened her eyes and placed her hands either side of his face, holding him steady, looking deep within him that he came—short, shallow thrusts within her, as their eyes held each other, deep within each other, just as their bodies were deep inside, connected, his seed given to her.

He kissed her mouth, then her cheeks, her throat, before rolling to one side and pulling her to him.

"Melisende." He sighed. "Melisende. Your name is so beautiful, like a prayer."

Her cheek was pressed against his chest, as if she was listening to the steady thump of his heart as it slowed down from the frenzy to its normal steady beat. She kissed his chest and looked up at him with laughter in her eyes. "And what, Sir Galien, would your prayers ask for, I wonder? A comfortable bed? A shelter through which the morning breeze doesn't blow?" He lifted a strand of her blonde hair up to the pale light, marvelling at its brilliance, and let it fall back down again. By the time he was ready to meet her gaze he knew that now was the time. Her smile fell in reaction to the look in his eyes. "What is it? What's wrong?"

"Nothing. Everything is absolutely right. You must come with me, Melisende. For I cannot consider leaving you behind."

She rolled away, until he could see only her profile, as she gazed up to the roof through which the first soft blush of morning was entering. He reached out and brought her hand within his. He could feel a tension within her that hadn't been there before. But there was no going back now, not on any level. The more he thought about her coming with him the more right it felt. He did not wait for her to speak.

"Last night shouldn't have happened, of course it shouldn't—you, a maid, and me, a wanted man. But it *did* happen and I, for one, cannot regret it. I love you, Melisende and I cannot be without you."

She withdrew her hand from his and lay quietly for one moment before swinging her legs to the ground. She reached for her gown. He watched in silence as she dressed. He swallowed. She still said nothing.

"I know I have nothing to give you. My life till this moment has been spent in the shadows. But that's all changed now, *changed* since I met you." He watched as she finished tying the laces at the sides of her dress, watched her as she opened the door and let in the fresh morning air. "Say something, Melisende."

But she stood stock still until he could bear it no longer. He rose and stood behind her, his hands running down the length of her arms before slipping around her slender waist. He followed her gaze out to the mudflats that lay to the north, stretched bloody in the red morning light.

"I cannot come with you, Galien."

He closed his eyes as if he'd been struck and his hands stilled on her waist. "Why not?"

"Because of something you told me when you first entered the priory. That you were a lone wolf, with no home, and would never have one. Galien, we're different you and I. I need a home. The Abbess... My work at the hospital... It's what I've wanted my whole life. It's the only home I know. The only place I've ever felt safe enough to be myself." She shook her head in emphasis. "I cannot leave. I simply cannot."

"Melisende. I can change. I'll settle, make a home for us."

"And you'd be happy doing that?" She shook her head. "I don't think so. I think marrying me would make you very *un*happy. You'd feel trapped, feel you'd let your family down, feel hatred instead of love for me."

"Do not tell me what *would*, or would *not*, make me happy!" He chewed his lip as he tried to rein in the flare of anger—fuelled, he knew, as much by fear that she may be right, as by frustration that she didn't believe him.

"I know that what you say is what you believe at this moment."

The anger dissipated at her quiet voice and became overwhelmed by a stronger fear—that he would leave this day and would never see her again. "I *want* you, Melisende. I want you beside me for the rest of my life. And I'll do anything it takes to make that happen. *That* is what I believe; *that* is the truth."

For one long moment before she spoke, Galien thought he might have convinced her. But with the shake of her head, his heart fell. "I cannot go."

"You do not love me then."

But she didn't have to speak for him to know he was wrong—the cloud of distress in her eyes told him everything he needed to know. "'Tis nothing to do with love. 'Tis to do with..."

"Fear." He finished her sentence that hung in the air searching for a truth he knew she could not acknowledge. He cupped her face in his hands and shook his head, trying to fathom why she could deny something that was blindingly obvious to him. He turned her in his arms so she was facing the horizon once more. "Look out there. *That's* where you belong, with me, out in the world, living, *free*. Not hidden away in the priory."

"Galien, don't you see? The priory *is* freedom to me. I can *think* there, I can practice medicine there, I can study and learn and *live* there. I cannot do those things as a wife."

"You can, as *my* wife." He turned her and kissed her gently. But he felt her stiffen in his arms and he drew away.

"I *cannot.*"

An icy cold determination gripped him. He would *not* lose her. "Then I shall stay. 'Tis clear. If you will not come with me, then I shall stay."

She jerked her head to his, panic in her eyes. "No! You cannot. You will be hunted down and killed by the King. You know he has no forgiveness in him, no mercy. 'Twould be a death sentence."

He shook his head. "The only death sentence for me would be to lose you. And *that*, I cannot do." He brought her close to him, clasped her head against his chest, intent on removing the panic and fear in her eyes, desperate to bring her as close to his heart as possible. "Melisende," he whispered against her hair as he kissed her. It was only when he fanned his hands over her back that he felt the telltale shudder of tears. He pulled her away and held her face up to his. "Melisende," he repeated.

She shook her head, unable to speak at first, as tears fell from her face. "I never thought," she gulped, "to *feel* like this."

"Well accept it, for I do." She stepped away, taking deep breaths as she tried to calm herself. He placed his hands on her shoulders, holding her there, not wanting her to move, as he searched her face for clues. But she had her eyes lowered. "Melisende. Come with me, for I will not leave without you."

He didn't dare move, simply waited. It was long moments before she expelled a deep breath and looked up at him with eyes that were both serious and sad. He frowned, fearing the worst.

"You must return to France, Galien. You must."

"There's only one way I'll do that. Will you come?"

She nodded slowly. "I'll come."

He gripped her shoulders, hardly daring to believe her words. "You will?"

She nodded again but her lips didn't turn into a smile. "I will."

He brought her tight against him and kissed the top of her head. "Thank you. I know you are afraid. 'Tis a brave decision but the only right one and I'll make sure you don't regret it."

She pulled away, a slight frown playing on her brow as she steadily regarded him. "I'll do whatever I have to do to keep you safe."

She turned away abruptly, the complex mix of frown and smile quickly gone as she glanced back at him. "Come we must eat, gather our strength. 'Twill be a hot day, we can bathe here in the creek. We will make the most of this last day together... *here...*"

There was something in the way she said those words—a note of regret, a poignancy—that caused him a brief moment of uncertainty. But, before he could say anything, she returned to him and lifted her chin until her lips were so close to his, he could feel her sweet breath upon his face.

"I love you, Galien." She reached up and swept away his uncertainty with a kiss.

CHAPTER TWELVE

The afternoon passed in a quiet, heated haze of love-making, swimming in the creek, and eking out the last of their bread and wine with the fresh seafood they found in the creek. But slowly, inexorably the sun followed its course until it hung on the western horizon, shedding its rich light over the flat expanse of marshes.

Melisende took one last look around the cottage that had witnessed their lovemaking and closed the door. Sadness overwhelmed her. She'd experienced magic here, a connection with another person, which she'd never again feel.

She turned to see Galien, standing at the edge of the clearing under the shelter of the wind-twisted trees that surrounded the old cob cottage, looking out at the horizon. With his broad shoulders, feet planted firmly beneath him, and one hand on his sword, he looked like a man ready for anything—a man in command. And she knew he was in command of her heart now, whether she liked it or not.

She walked up to him and he drew her to his side. "'Tis like the mudflats are on fire."

She followed his gaze. "They've come alive. Like me."

He nodded. "Like a spark from a tinder box on grass spent too long without water, it consumes." He paused. "It also renews." She shivered and he turned her in his arms so she faced him. "My love, what is the matter?"

"I'm scared, Galien. I'm so scared." It was the truth, but not for the reason he believed.

"There's nothing to be scared about, my love. We will be together from now on."

She felt a sharp pang of regret. "I love you, Galien. And I always will."

He frowned. "Melisende, there is sadness in your voice. I know I am asking you to leave your home but we will be together. You must have no fear, for I will care for you well."

She nodded and forced herself to smile. "Come, we must be at the beach soon. This will be our last chance for weeks. We must go."

They emerged from the dark channel, hidden by the tall reeds, out onto the exposed and windy sand spit. The moon had risen above the inland hills, showering the scene with a strange silvery light. Before them, men crouched, sheltering in the lee of the sand banks that formed the only high ground at the tip of the remote sand spit. Around the men were corricles, while yet others stood before empty seaweed carts. They nodded in silent greeting to Melisende and cast brief, suspicious glances at Galien, before turning their gaze once more back to the sea.

"Who are these people, Melisende?"

"Regulars. I know them all." She glanced around. "But I don't see Tom. He's usually here." She frowned. "Mayhap he was delayed."

"So 'tis safe?"

"Aye. They are waiting for the boats to arrive. The carts are to transport the casks of wine and brandy back to the village. And from there to all parts of Norfolk. 'Tis hard but profitable work for these men. They're amply rewarded for their risk."

"A great risk indeed. They'll be easy targets if the excise men discover them."

"Aye. But the local men do not follow the usual paths. They travel across the marshes on ancient tracks that avoid the treacherous mud that would swallow a man whole. And besides, the road by which the excise men would approach is well guarded."

They walked towards the man holding the lanthorn. The other men clustered around him, all peering out to the distant horizon.

"Any word?" asked Melisende.

"Only word is that strangers have been seen heading to port." The man's face was grim in the strange light.

"Strangers?" She shrugged. "Might be anyone."

The man turned and spat out the root he was chewing. "Might be. Might not be."

But Melisende knew. She had a gut feeling and glanced at Galien whose face reflected her fears. "But you came anyway?"

"I have men who'll give us warning if needs be." His gaze remained steadily on the black sea. "And who's that with you?"

"A priest. He needs passage on a returning boat."

He glanced at Galien, his eyes dark but penetrating dots in the creased and weathered skin. She reached inside her cloak and withdrew a bag and gave it to him. He weighed it in his hand, judging its worth. She held her breath. He pocketed the coin and she exhaled.

"You have another bag of coin for the captain?"

"Aye," Melisende answered, her heart in her mouth. "There is no problem?"

"If there is sufficient coin, there is never a problem."

She returned to Galien. "Now all we have to do is wait."

The man looked around and lit the lanthorn, placing his back against the wind. The men shuffled closer, their movements quickening at sight of the light. All eyes were strained on an answering signal out to sea. There was none. The man snuffed out the light and they waited for an interminable amount of time before repeating the exercise. This time there was an answering flash at sea and slowly, the shape of two boats could be seen, lighter than the dark sea, moving towards them.

"Mel—my lady!" Melisende turned to find Tom standing breathless before her. He pulled off his hat. "My lady." And turned to Galien and nodded.

She reached out to him, for his eyes looked scared. "What is it?"

"My lady, the Abbess sends word to Father Galien. The King's men have been and gone. She says they did not find what they were looking for and wishes you God's speed."

Galien exchange a glance with Melisende. "And they are all well? No-one was hurt?"

The man looked uncomfortable. "The Lady Abbess told me not to say."

"Tell me. I will not betray your words."

"There was a fight and injuries resulted." Melisende gasped. "But not many and the Abbess was untouched. 'Tis under control and not so bad as you imagine. Ada is looking after them well."

She turned to Galien. "I must go to them."

Galien reached out and took Melisende's arm, holding her tight. "No! You heard Tom. They are managing and Ada is capable. You've taught her well. She will deal with this."

"She is still young."

"As young as you were, no doubt, when you first started working at the hospital. Listen to me, Melisende. There will always be reasons to return. Always. You have to put our love first."

She stepped back as the first of the two row boats surged in on a wave. "I *am* putting our love first, Galien. I can't bear the thought of your love for me turning into frustration, anger and eventually hate, as you realize you've traded your dreams for the dull domesticity of a wife and children. You'd hate that life. And 'tis a home for which I crave. We want different things, you and I."

He shook his head, determinedly and turned to greet the captain who'd jumped out of the boat and accepted the money from Galien.

"'Tis for two," Galien said firmly.

"Aye, then," said the captain, "we leave in minutes. 'Tis not safe. Last night we saw men heading to the beach. 'Twas not excise men though."

A shiver ran through Melisende. They must have been the men seeking Galien. 'Twas even more imperative that he go. She had to do something to make him see, to make him escape the danger that lurked on shore.

While men moved briskly back and forward, loading their goods onto the waiting carts and boats, Galien held out his hand for Melisende who stood transfixed, unable to believe what she was about to do.

There was a muffled shout as a second boat was pulled to shore to offload its cargo.

"Melisende," Galien called as loud as he could above the noise of the men and the surf, but she took a step backwards. He came after her. "The captain says it's now or never. Come." He grasped her hand.

But she pulled back. "You go, Galien. I cannot."

He took hold of both her hands and his expression was fierce. "I'll stay, then. For I won't leave you."

"You must go." Desperation rose, clawing at her chest, her throat, making it difficult to breathe, difficult to utter the lies. "I don't *want* you here, Galien. Don't you see? I don't *want* you!" The shrillness in her last words tore into her soul, just as she could see it ripped into Galien's heart.

He let go of her hands and stumbled back from her, the water surging up around his legs.

"Go!" She called out but the words were swept away. She turned away, unable to witness the pain in his eyes, and not wanting him to see the tears in hers. She waited long moments before turning to watch the boat move away to the larger boat anchored off shore. He had his back to her and didn't turn around.

A wave broke over Melisende's ankles, soaking the hem of her cloak. Then another wave and then another were between her and Galien, and then he was swallowed into the darkness.

She staggered back. She'd run through the arguments in her head all night and all day. They wanted opposite things—her, the peace and stability of a home in which she could study, could learn, could be herself. And he? He had his own dreams to follow which had nothing to do with security. It was madness to leave the safety of the priory. She looked inland to where the priory lay, waiting for her.

It was as if life was held in the balance. The balance was heavily weighted in favour of returning to the priory. But what of other things? What of her newly awakened body, what of her heart that ached with a throbbing hurt when Galien had finally released his hand from hers? What of that?

Doubt ebbed and flowed within her, like the waves which surged around her ankles. If she wanted stability so much, then why, as Galien had asked, did she risk so much in joining with the smugglers? Was it because deep down, it *wasn't* safety that she wanted, but excitement?

Galien was the unknown, he was life—passion and feeling—everything she'd always believed she didn't want. But the truth was that she'd been pushing the boundaries of her freedom with her hospital work and with the smuggling, believing she did it solely for the good of others. She wanted to help people, of course she did, but she now recognized the restless spirit and thirst for adventure that was her true nature—a nature she hadn't been able to accept before forced into it by the prospect of life without the man she loved. She no more wanted a cloistered life than Galien.

So what was she going to do?

She turned to watch the second boat push back into the surf and knew she had no choice. The decision had been made for her.

CHAPTER THIRTEEN

Galien gripped the weathered rough wood of the boat's gunwhale, and look out to the black horizon. Always before he'd known his destination. But now he felt nothing but emptiness before him.

He'd done what he'd set out to do, all those months before, but he was leaving England feeling the reverse. He'd left things undone. He'd left a part of himself there. And there was nothing he could do about it. He loved Melisende but he had no right to demand that she come with him. She was searching for something as he was also, and she'd said she'd found it at Blakesmere Priory. He had no right to rob her of her sense of belonging, of the only place she called home.

But... he looked up to the vast sky, studded with stars, and closed his eyes against their brightness, feeling his eyes smart. But... the thought of life without her was unimaginable. His next step was to report to the King of France, to continue the work he'd begun so many years before, after his family's murder. But for all the justness of his cause, he felt the energy had been lanced and there was nothing but emptiness within. How the hell was he going to survive without her?

The boat surged gently on the rolling seas. He felt a jolt as the second boat knocked into the side of the bigger boat. The men spoke in quiet undertones as they moved around the deck, lashing the smaller boats into position. He could almost hear his name being called, as if from far away. He shook his head. He was going mad now, haunted by her sweet voice.

Then he felt the touch of a hand on his arm. He stilled. It was no rough grip of a seaman. He spun round. The clouds scudded past, revealing a lopsided moon that made her blonde hair and the whites of her eyes shine. She was ethereal, a figment of his desperate imagination. Her hood had fallen, pushed away by the incessant wind, her hair whipped around her face, as if she were some valkyrie. But her eyes held his with a passion he recognized.

He groaned and reached out for her, pulling her to him, his lips finding hers in an instant. And they weren't the lips of a phantom, they were real, warm and moving against his with a passion equal to his. He kissed her cheeks, her hair, her lips once more and then simply held her against him, allowing his senses to make her real to him.

"Melisende, Melisende, Melisende," he murmured into her hair. "Can it be you?" He pulled away from her and held her head between his hands, searching her face. She gave a long, low laugh.

"If 'tis not, you must have just kissed a sailor."

He laughed and rested his forehead against hers, twisting to watch the oars as they began to pound in unison into the white-flecked ocean. "We are under way now, Melisende. There is no going back. I will make a home for us."

"No," she shook her head. "I don't want a home. I want to be with you. *With* you, wherever that may be. I would not have you tamed."

"Are you sure?"

"I'm only sure of one thing." Her finger was hesitant, darted softly from his lips, cheeks, brow, as if she, too, was making sure he was real. "That when you left me, you took everything that made sense with you. I was left with nothing after you'd gone."

"But Blakesmere, the Abbess, what of them?"

She glanced down as a shadow of sorrow passed over her features. "I love them, I'll miss them, but it's you I can't live without."

He brought her into his arms and held her tight against his body. Only then did he feel her shiver, and become aware of the wet of her cloak seeping into his clothes.

"Come, let's go to the forecastle, we'll have some shelter from the wind there."

Behind the sheet of leather and wooden shelter, he took off his cloak and draped it around her and drew her into his arms, sheltering her from the weather. He felt as if was holding the most precious thing on earth.

Melisende felt strangely at peace in his arms. Now the decision was made, she knew it was the right one, despite the raging seas and the fact she had no idea if she'd ever see her home, her sisters and the woman who'd been a mother to her, again.

In his arms, she was sheltered from everything. She knew no matter where he took her, roaming the world, or finding a home, she had her home with him. Slowly they slipped into an uneasy sleep, awoken only by the rolling of the boat on the lively swell of the sea. The shape of the flat coast of Holland lay before them. They rose and walked to the deck where they could watch the port grow larger.

He lifted her face to his. "You look sad, Melisende. Tell me, you do not regret your decision already?"

She shook her head. "Nay, I just wish I could have spoken one last time to the Abbess, made her understand."

Galien patted the pocket in his cloak. "Ah, but I nearly forgot, Lady Anne gave me a package to open once I was safely out of England."

"Really? Where is it?"

He reached in his leathern bag and drew out a package. "She asked me to take this to France. She wanted me to open it in sight of the coast. Something sentimental no doubt, about her homeland."

Melisende frowned. "Sentimental? The Abbess? I never knew her to be sentimental about anything. I wonder what it can be?"

He smiled and kissed her. "Only one way to find out." He broke the seal, scanned it and then passed it to her to read. "It's for you."

My dearest Melisende,

If you are reading this then you'll have made your decision. And I believe it to be a good one.

I sensed from your first meeting with Sir Galien, your attraction to each other. He is a good man, from a good family. His only fault is his fierce passion for everything, and everyone, he holds dear. But it is this fault which I know will ensure that he cares for you always. I pray to God he finds peace with you and can turn away from the bitterness of revenge.

You have a home with me at Blakesmere, always. But I believe you will live a fuller life, one that will serve God better. My dear, whatever life brings to you, face it with the same courage and compassion you always have.

Send word where you are and I will send your books to you. Your work here will be carried on, but your books and knowledge will go with you and I have no doubt that you will do good in the world with it. With Sir Galien by your side.

God bless you.

Your loving aunt...

"She knew..." Melisende folded the parchment carefully as she tried to hold back the tears. "She knew I'd come with you and she said nothing to stop me."

"As I said, she's a wise woman. She knows you and she knows me... knows that I'll care for you now and for always." He captured both her hands in his and brought them to his lips. "Will you marry me, Melisende? Will you be my wife and be with me, by my side, whatever happens?"

She swallowed down the huge lump that had appeared from nowhere and nodded. "I love you, heart and soul, and I *will* be your wife."

"Then we are married. We will have the marriage blessed in France as soon as we've landed."

He dipped his head to hers and kissed her briefly. He started to move away but she thrust her fingers through his hair, and pressed her lips to his. As they kissed she could feel the deck pitch and roll beneath her feet, could feel the keen wind on her face, and she knew their future lay before them, unknown and unknowable. But so long as he stood beside her, she could face anything, and she wanted nothing more.

THE END

Awakening
Book 3—Angelique

CHAPTER ONE

North Norfolk Coast, England, 1214

Lady Angelique Gresham barely felt the chill rain that descended through the ruined chapel roof onto her upturned face. She blinked her eyes to clear the water that clung to her lashes, but dared make no further movement, other than to tighten her grip around the silver dagger.

Someone was out there, on the black, rain-soaked marsh. No one should be.

It was too wild a night for man or beast to roam the desolate land between castle and sea. Only a foolish woman would have ventured forth for sentimental reasons—only a foolish woman, whose regret at her impulsive behaviour deepened with each pounding beat of her heart.

Angelique focused all her senses on locating the shadow that had just passed by the window. She strained to hear any sign of life above the whine of the wind as it caught the jagged edges of the chapel's flint walls, but she heard no other sound. Her eyes scanned the darkness for movement, but she saw nothing but shadows of stone, black against the charcoal sky.

She exhaled shakily—not realizing she'd been holding her breath—and edged her way to the gaping hole where the door had once been. She *had* to return to the castle. No one would hear her cries from here. No one knew where she was. It had been a mistake to come.

She hesitated under the stone arch, narrowing her eyes in an effort to give form to the shadows outside the chapel walls. Suddenly, the shadows coalesced and before she could raise her dagger, her hand was clamped by a man's hand, and her body was brought tight against a man's body. She struggled to draw breath to scream, but a calloused hand closed tight against her mouth.

"Angel!" His voice was low, strong and insistent. "By Christ, will you be still!"

Despite the blast of energy that gave her the strength to struggle against his vice-like grip, she suddenly stilled, responding to his voice before her mind had time to inform her body of what it was already aware. She knew this man.

He loosened his grip and she twisted around, hardly daring to believe what her senses were telling her. In the darkness and rain she could see nothing: only feel his warm breath upon her face. Her nostrils flared as her body reacted to his scent. It *was* him.

She raised her hand to his face, touching it hesitantly, still unable to believe that he had returned after all these years. His hand slipped from her mouth and rested on her shoulders.

"Guy?" Her hushed voice was swept away by the wind, but she knew he'd heard. She could feel the heat of his fingers, despite the thick, fur-lined cloak, as they pressed briefly against her shoulders. His hand covered hers before he twisted her palm to his lips and kissed it. A shiver of desire rippled through her body.

"The same."

A cry emerged from some hidden place deep within and she dropped her head to his chest, squeezing her eyes tight shut, finding the reality of him stronger that way, fearing he would disappear like he did in her dreams. But he didn't. Instead, his arms swept around her and pulled her close.

For one long moment she allowed the warmth of his hands to penetrate her body, too long cold; for one long moment she absorbed his presence as if it were an extension of her own, and for one long moment she felt as if anything were possible.

But then reality filtered through her shocked senses. She shook her head and slid her hands up against his chest holding him at bay. He would go from her, like he always had, her dreams reflecting his disappearance nine years before. She couldn't allow his leaving to hurt her again. She couldn't risk losing herself in him.

"Why are you here?"

"To see you."

His powerful voice had softened and she could hear emotion in the timbre of his words. But she shook her head once more and stepped away. His fingers slowly unfurled from her cloak, as if reluctant to release her.

"Why? What do you want with me?"

"I wish to see you, to talk with you, to find out how you fare." He reached out to touch her cheek but she shook her head, tilting her face up to his in an attitude of defiance she hoped would make him keep his distance. If he didn't, she'd be lost. It must have worked because he let his hand fall back to his side. "But not here. Come, I will escort you back. The marsh is a chill and pitiless place to greet an old friend."

An old friend. That was all she was to him. "Of course."

She turned and walked swiftly down the narrow path that led to the castle, aware of his presence just one step behind. Her mind raced, trying to catch up with the surge of emotions and reactions that flooded her body. Was he really here to see her? If so, what did he want from her?

They entered the castle by the postern gate, which she'd left unbarred for her return. There was a small group of guards talking and drinking by the gatehouse but they didn't notice them pass. She led him up the outer steps of the keep to the Great Hall.

Once inside the dimly lit Hall, she scanned it to see if Guy had brought others, to see if anything had changed. But it was just as she'd left it. The fresh rushes, laid by the servants before they'd departed to attend the Charter Fair earlier that day, the dying embers of a fire and an old, deaf dog, half asleep, who flicked his tail in lazy welcome.

"Where is everyone?"

She started at the closeness of his voice behind her and walked away, busying herself with lighting the other rush lights, her hand trembling as she held up a lighted taper to the tallow. It sputtered into life, the flames flickering over the unadorned whitewashed flint walls. She drew in a deep breath and turned to face him.

"My steward, Sir Richard, and the rest of my servants are celebrating in the town after the Charter Fair. Probably sleeping it off by now."

"Leaving you alone? Why did you allow it?"

She plucked off her cloak and draped it over a wooden bench to dry, still with her back to him. "Because I am safe. My guards are at the main gate."

"They didn't even notice you coming in through the postern gate."

"They assumed it was barred. I'd slipped out for a few minutes only and at high tide the castle causeway will be impassable. Anyway, I think it is a little late for you to worry about my safety."

She glanced at the trestle table on the dais where supper for one was laid out. "I'm sorry, I'm not prepared for company."

"I want nothing, Angel. Just to talk."

"You must have wine." She opened a large solid chest and plucked out another mazer cup, keeping her eyes down, still unable to meet his gaze. "The silver cups are already packed, I'm afraid."

"Packed? You are going somewhere?"

She nodded, but refused to elaborate. "Are you hungry? You must have been riding long and hard. I have some supper here. I hope it's enough." She brought the food to the table before the fire and laid it out, her eyes cast down, as if busy checking that all was in order for their supper.

"Stop, Angel, turn to me."

She returned to the chest and took her time searching its contents. "There is more food in here somewhere. You should have told me you were coming. How far have you travelled, did you say?" She could hear herself babbling but she couldn't stop. Never in her wildest dreams had she expected to see Guy de Lacey again.

"I didn't."

"Well, it must have been far. We are so isolated here. You—"

Suddenly she felt his hands run up her arms. She closed her eyes tight and the lid of the chest slipped from her hands and banged shut.

"Stop, Angel." He turned her to face him and brought his hand to her chin and lifted it. "Stop. Look at me."

Slowly she opened her eyes, keeping her gaze lowered to his mouth— the softness of his lips was separated by a firm, uncompromising line. She frowned. That sternness was new. Her gaze lifted to his cheeks, roughened with stubble. He must have been riding long hours, not to have shaved. She touched his face, she couldn't help herself.

"The texture of your skin, your hair, it's different, it's changed." Her fingertips scraped against the stubble, tracing a path that took her back to his lips.

"Nine years brings changes to a man."

"And to a woman."

His head moved under her hand. "No. Not to you."

She looked up into his eyes then. Hazel eyes that glowed golden, reflecting the jumping flames of the rush lights that were beginning to lick into the cold air, consuming it and giving them strength. Just like him, she thought. If she let him, he'd consume her. And she couldn't risk that.

She turned her back to him—drawing a deep, ragged breath as she went—and busied herself pouring wine into each cup. "I've changed, Guy. And you mustn't think otherwise. Please, be seated. You must be hungry and tired."

"I was, but am no more. Not now I have you to feast my eyes on."

She heard him step behind her and she froze, unable to move, even as his hands captured the long strands of hair that had escaped her widow's coif. She closed her eyes as he wrapped her curls around his fingers, drawing his hand closer to her head with each sinuous movement. She tensed as his fingers fumbled briefly with her coif and net before her hair was freed, and tumbled into his waiting hands. He lifted her hair to one side, his breath, hot against her neck.

Heat pooled in her stomach revealing a long-forgotten desire that she'd presumed dead. That it was still alive shocked her into movement. She put down the cups of wine that her trembling hands threatened to spill and turned to him, her hair falling around her face, untamed and tousled by his hands.

"It's your turn to stop. Now! Don't you dare turn you charm on me again, Guy. You think you can return here and seduce me after all these years? You think I've been waiting for this?" Her breathing was coming in short, sharp pants, aroused by his proximity and by the frustration that he'd waited so long to come to her.

A faint smile flickered on his lips and in his eyes. "Maybe." He brushed his thumb across her cheek. "Your face is flushed, your eyes bright."

She took his hands and flung them away. "Through anger, Guy. Anger! I want no one. There's only one thing I want now."

His eyes narrowed but his smile lingered. "Just one thing? You are easy to please, my lady. Tell me what it is you want and I'll give it to you."

She bit her lip and shook her head. "'Tis not so easily given."

His smile faded. "Tell me. What is it you want?"

"My freedom."

CHAPTER TWO

He shook his head. "Freedom." His whisper left a trail of goose bumps across her skin. "Who amongst us has that?"

She swallowed. "I do. Or I will. I repeat, Guy. I will *not* be seduced."

Despite her determination to meet his eye, to convince him she was speaking the truth, she had to turn away first. She picked up the cup of wine and held it out to him, cursing her trembling hand that would do nothing to help convince him of the veracity of her words.

He took the wine and sipped it, his eyes still watching her intently. "What have I done to make you think I wish to seduce you?" His eyes sparkled in the light. "Your hair is damp. I was merely freeing it from its bonds so it could dry."

"So considerate." She sipped her own wine. "You would have me believe you've changed so much?" She shook her head. "I cannot."

His face was suddenly serious. "I was ever considerate of you. Of only you."

"So considerate you would declare your love for me and then leave me without a word." She sat down in an armchair, her fingers brushing the silky smooth carvings, whose design was muted by age. "Please take a seat."

She wondered if he'd even heard her as he continued to stand, leaning against the fire lintel, the ruddy glow of the flames illuminating his suddenly tense features. A muscle flickered in his jaw. "I had no choice but to leave. I had nothing to give you."

"I wanted nothing."

"You didn't know *what* you wanted. You were young. But I *knew* what you wanted, what you deserved. And it was more than the nothing you'd have got if you'd married me. Your father would have disinherited you; he would never have allowed us to marry. He wanted you to marry a man of wealth."

A cold stillness swept through her veins. It was as if a night had fallen that would never break. "I had no care for what my father wanted. He had no love for me. I would have trusted you with my life then, Guy. I offered you my life but you turned it down. You wanted adventure and excitement more than you wanted me."

He shook his head. "I did what I thought best. I left so you could have a better life."

"Better?" The word was barely audible through the bitterness that choked her. "Well it *is* now my husband is dead. I earned my wealth and now I intend to keep it. I have my lands and my dower, thanks to the King."

He frowned. "I was wrong. You've changed. You were never so mercenary, so unfeeling."

"*You* try and be caring about a man who abused me in the vilest way. *You* try and regret the death of a man whose only pleasure was in the pain he inflicted on others. I am glad he died. Because if he hadn't, I would have."

He reached out to her but Angelique slapped his arm and turned away, unable to look into his eyes because of the painful memories that flooded her mind.

"I didn't know—"

"How could you? No one but my closest servants knew. He took great pains to pretend he was a good man to everyone else."

"I would have returned."

"No you wouldn't."

His hazel eyes turned fiery and his hand shot out and held hers with a grip, from which she couldn't have pulled away, even if she'd wanted to. And faced with the full strength of him, she didn't want to. He'd broadened in the years since she'd seen him. Always tall, he now had the breadth to make him undeniably a powerful man. The hand that gripped hers was large, the muscles in his forearm bunched under tanned skin.

"Woman, stop your recriminations and listen."

"I'm listening. Tell me why you're here. Tell me what your purpose is."

"I've told you what my purpose is. I've come to see you."

"Why?"

"The King has rewarded me well for my years fighting with him in France. And you are free now. I want you."

"You want me." She nodded to herself, feeling her anger rising. "No, what you want is to own me. I know men now. I know what they want."

His eyes were black under his lowering brow, full of anger and frustration.

"Don't presume to judge me by your knowledge of another, Angel." His voice filled the Hall, as if he were commanding a legion of unruly soldiers, and his eyes held hers with an angry intensity that cut right through to her heart. She heard the hurt as well as the anger in his voice. But even if she hadn't, she knew what he felt, because she felt it too.

Alongside the anger and hurt at the past, there rose a clawing, uncivilized need for him that went beyond understanding. It shortened her breath, it made her heart pound loudly in her ears and sent shards of desire skittering through her body, heating and melting as they went. It was as if the flint walls had receded leaving only the two of them, alone in the world. It was a madness from which she had to turn away.

She tore her gaze from his and jumped up, shaking her head. She couldn't succumb to these feelings. She had too much to lose. She inhaled a long, slow breath, desperate to regain her senses before she turned back to face him. "I shall judge as I see fit."

He sighed sharply. "You're wrong. I don't want to own you." He stepped towards her. "Angel, don't you understand? I want to marry you."

For a long moment, she was stunned into silence. Then memories of her life with her husband came crashing back, one after another, image upon image of the humiliation and misery of her marriage. "Same thing."

"It doesn't have to be."

"Yes it does. If I marry you I have no rights. You have control over me, over my lands. Why would I want to marry you? I have no need, no requirement to be married. I *know* marriage. And I want no more of it."

He reached over to her and pulled her to him. His chest heaved against her breasts as he inhaled. Her own breathing came quickly, like a trapped animal sensing the worst. He moved his hands down the sides of her body and around her back, pulling her even closer to him. "What happened to you, Angel?"

She closed her eyes in relief, instantly stilling under the comfort of his embrace and warmth of his voice. "Life happened," she whispered. He was so close now. "I married. I grew up." She looked up at him, sad at the gulf of understanding that existed between them, despite their physical closeness. "I wish for no more marriage, Guy."

"But I hear the King wishes you to marry."

She smiled then, for the first time. "I have come to an arrangement with the King. I have paid for my freedom."

Just saying it gave her the strength to pull away from him and sit down. She indicated once more that he should be seated in the chair opposite. He searched her eyes for a long moment before sitting down heavily in the carved chair. He picked up his wine and took a long drink, his eyes never leaving hers. His presence pressed against her as surely as his hands had.

She did not drink but returned his gaze levelly, with the strength gained from years of assuming an impassive face before her jealous husband.

He frowned into his cup. "You have great trust in the King."

"And you are saying you do not? You are on dangerous ground."

"We all live our lives on dangerous ground, Angel. There is no such thing as safety."

She swallowed. It could not be so. "Maybe not. But we have to try to make our lives as safe as possible. I *have* to trust the King because he holds my life in his hands."

"'Tis not enough reason to trust, my Lady Angelique. You were ever want to trust the wrong person."

"I trusted you." She sat back against her chair, suddenly needing its support. "Was that wrong?"

"You trusted me to give you something I could not give."

She shrugged. "A woman has little choice in the matter of whom to trust. Besides this time, the trust is bought—which will make it far more reliable."

He leaned forward to her, his eyes hot and urgent. "Listen to me, Angelique. What the King wants, the King gets. You are too valuable to him. He will sell you—and the freedom you value so much—to the highest bidder, whether for money or power. And he's hungry for both." He sat back again. "Question is, not *whether* you will marry, but *who.*"

CHAPTER THREE

It was what she'd heard, it was what she'd feared, but it was what, up 'till now, she'd refused to believe.

She shook her head. "No, it cannot be." She rose and paced away from the fire, her leather shoes muffled upon the rush-strewn floor. "It cannot be," she murmured to herself, willing the resolve, the strength, to return. She turned to him again. It was easier from a distance. "It cannot be, Guy."

He didn't move, as if sensing her need for distance. "It can be."

"So"—she felt reassured by his restraint, and returned to the fire and took her seat once more—"you are suggesting I marry *you* to prevent a marriage arranged by the King?"

"That is not the only reason I am suggesting it, I—"

She held up her hand, needing him to stop. "The King would never approve it. Besides I shall never again marry. I am my own woman now. I have my independence. Or will have. The King has agreed to it, provided I give him his price."

"Oh, Angel." Guy looked at her with weary eyes. "*You* are an innocent."

"Maybe. But 'tis not the only thing I'm relying on. Once his envoy has arrived to take the silver, I will leave for the north."

Guy nodded, but she could see he was not convinced she would escape the King's reach. "Aye. It would have been a good plan, if..." He shrugged and trailed off, apparently unwilling to tell her why her plan would fail. And she didn't ask him. She couldn't. She couldn't bear knowing her plans might fail.

"So tell me," she said brightly, needing to change the subject, needing to find a footing between them that was untainted by fear, recrimination or the compulsion she felt to reach out and touch him, to connect with his body in any way she could. "Tell me what you have been doing. Last time I saw you, you were leaving for France."

"There is little more to be said."

"But what of the battles you fought beside the King? There is nothing to be said about them?"

He looked at her sadly, cradling his cup of wine in his hands as he looked back at the fire. "Nothing I wish to say."

"You used to talk of nothing else but your desire to see other lands, to test yourself against others in battle."

"I was young and knew no better." He sighed and returned his gaze to her once more. "Now I do. There was too much death, too much darkness."

"But you prospered."

"Aye, I prospered. I did well enough so that I never have to return. And, God willing, I never shall."

She frowned. "You seem to have everything worked out."

"That depends. And not upon God." He put down his cup and leaned forward and took her hands. She tried to keep a cool head but was aware of every pressure, every slide of his fingers against hers. "Sweet Jesus, Angel, do you know how long I've imagined this moment?"

Her mouth was dry as she tried to form the words. Yes, she did, for it was the same with her. But she could say nothing. For whatever went on in her imagination had little connection to the harsh reality of life. She shook her head.

"No? I've been imagining this moment since the last time I saw you, on your wedding day. You looked so beautiful."

"You were not there. I did not see you."

"I was there, watching. I needed to see with my own eyes that you were married and unobtainable. And you were; you'd moved beyond me. I couldn't believe I'd ever had the courage to kiss you, to hold you."

The flickering flames of the fire suddenly seemed too potent as a wave of heat swept through her body. She could feel his lips upon hers, could feel the strength of his arms pulling her tight against his aroused body, as if it were yesterday.

"Nine years has made your memory unreliable. It was I, Sir Guy, who kissed you." She licked her lips as her heart quickened at the visceral surge of memories. "I waited until you were alone in the stables. Then I slipped my hands around you and forced you to press your body to mine. 'Twas I who reached up and pulled your head to mine so I could taste your lips." She watched with satisfaction as his eyes flashed darkly in response to her words. "Trust a man to turn his memory to his advantage."

"A forward lady, who always got what she wanted. I remember well, no matter what you say." His voice was roughened, like the stippled surface of the German Sea below which deep currents swirled.

She looked down, as the subsequent memories clouded her mind. "Sometimes I got what I didn't want. Marriage for instance. I never wanted that. I couldn't believe father had won and I was being wed."

"You always knew he had to win. You had no choice. Not then, and not now."

She shook her head. "Times change. My father died some years past— his land divided between my sisters and me—and my husband is dead. The death of these two men has brought me power."

He shook his head with a sadness in his eyes that made her uncomfortable. But then his eyes warmed again as they roamed her face: from her hair, to her eyes, cheeks and neck and lower. Her lips parted in response to the boldness of his stare, but then his gaze suddenly returned to her eyes and she froze, by instinct, like an animal caught in a predator's sight.

"Some things never change. Like you. You're still as beautiful as ever."

Suddenly instead of wanting to keep her distance, she wanted him near, she wanted him to see her for what she'd become. "Come, look closer in my eyes. Is that what you really see? Because it's not what I *feel*."

She took his hand and held it to her cheek, revelling in the feel of his strong, calloused palm against her delicate skin. As his eyes roamed her face, heat swept outwards from her centre, like the ripples from a stone dropped into a millpond.

"I see you still."

"But—"

"No. I see *you*, the real *you*, the one you keep hidden from the world. I see that person, unchanged since the day I first saw you."

He didn't move his hand, but continued to gaze at her. Tears, that had lain unshed for so many years, pressed against her hot eyes as she met his gaze.

"No. Guy, please don't. I'm here only for a few more nights—until the King's money is paid— and then I'll be leaving for the north where the Barons no longer support the King. I'll be safer there. You're right. I don't trust him. I don't trust anyone. I need to go where I cannot easily be reached."

"So I have only a few days and nights to persuade you to marry me?"

She inhaled tightly as she felt the touch of his lips against her fingers. "No. Only one night. You must be gone before my household return in the morn. Otherwise it could jeopardize my plans."

"One night. 'Tis all I need."

"So sure?"

His smile reflected her own, revealing their mutual understanding. Suddenly, the long, empty years that stood between them dissolved into nothing more than a heartbeat.

"Yes. That is all I need to show you that you should marry me."

She hesitated for a moment. She would never again be married. She wanted none of it. But she remembered the cravings of her body for this man beside her. She felt them still as he touched her, awakening within her feelings that she must forever suppress if she were to be in control of her life. Should she? Should she submit to this one weakness, this one night? One night in which to indulge herself, to explore herself, before closing down that side of her forever?

It was madness. "Even if you did persuade me to marry you—which you won't—the King would never allow it. You must go now, before the high tide makes the causeway impassable."

She started to stand but he stopped her.

"I'm not going. I will be with you this night if it's the last thing I do."

"If the King discovers you are alone with me, it might very well be your last."

"I'll risk it to show you what pleasure I can bring you."

"Pleasure outside marriage, not with the aim of bringing children into the world, is unholy. That is what the priests say."

"And you believe that?"

"No. If the priests believe what my husband did to me was good, then they are mistaken."

"So give me this night together."

She nodded slowly. Deep down inside her, where her mind seemed to hold no sway, the words formed, sprung from her body's needs.

"The night is yours."

He rose from the chair and extended his hand to hers in invitation. "Come to me, Angel."

CHAPTER FOUR

She flexed her hands as she tried to prevent herself from reaching out to him, to stop herself from slipping her fingers into his hair and pulling his face to hers, until his lips were pressed hard against hers. She swallowed and tentatively reached out to his hand. She could no more have prevented it than have stopped the spring tides rolling onto the marshes. He curled his fingers around hers and tugged her to him.

Her heart quickened as her hand pressed against his chest to balance herself. But she didn't pull away. Instead, she splayed her fingers over his chest, moving over the rough wool of his shirt, sensing the taut strength of his muscle that lay beneath. His muscles contracted under her touch as he sucked in a sharp breath. She looked up into his dark eyes. "I am here. What now?"

He lifted her chin and smiled as he brushed his lips against hers, so gently, so at odds with the power she could sense in his tense body. He held his mouth there, as if breathing her in, then he touched them with a delicacy and restraint she had no memory of, before drawing back, too soon.

"You won't regret it." His voice was husky with desire. He reached down, took her hand and brought it to his lips. "Now I'm going to show you how much I love you."

She gasped lightly, and bit her lips in a vain attempt to stop them trembling. He laughed and swept his lips over her knuckles. She frowned. "Why do you laugh?"

"Because I cannot believe I am here with you now. Besides, love does not have to be a solemn thing." His smile broadened. "Do you remember those games we used to play?"

She smiled as the memories of the two of them in the stables and then later, in the old chapel, came flooding back. "I might have forced you to kiss me but from there it was you who took the initiative, I remember well."

He grinned, a slow grin that made her stomach tighten with pleasure. It was the same smile of old, except the lines that bracketed his mouth and that fanned out from around his eyes, were deeper in the sun-browned skin. "Because I had no choice. Just one taste of your lips and I knew I had to explore the rest of your body, see if it tasted as good."

Lust ground, deep and needy, inside her. "Just as well we were only ever alone for moments at a time."

"Aye, stolen moments during which I would discover one part of your body at a time." He touched her shoulder and shifted her hair slightly, pushing her gown away a little. "Like your shoulder." His gaze narrowed as his finger caressed the dips and hollows around her shoulder. "Such delicacy." He looked up and caught her equally hot gaze. "And such strength."

She licked her lips. "I wasn't so strong when it came to us. It was you who rationed our time, limited our discoveries."

"We would have been found out, otherwise."

"But we weren't," she said softly.

"No thanks to you, Angel. You had no thought beyond us."

"No. I would have given you anything you wanted."

His smile was tense with desire and regret. "And now?"

She hesitated, knowing he wanted more than she could give. "We have this night. Only this night."

He nodded, and she could see in his eyes that he understood. But then he always had. "And we have something, now, Angel, that we longed for when we were young. A chamber to ourselves."

She shivered as his hand drew lazily up her spine. "All we had then was the old chapel."

"It was always so cold," he breathed against her cheek, teasing her senses.

She shivered. "And uncomfortable."

"Aye, no soft surfaces to lay you down on. And no doors, or windows. It was probably just as well the old chapel gave us little privacy, else—"

"Who knows what might have happened," she interrupted.

"*I* know what would have happened. Let me show you." He sat back down on the ornately carved armchair and pulled her onto his lap. His eyes flickered around her face, before settling on her lips. His fingers swept round her neck, and then down to her jaw, before curling under her chin. He tilted it up to meet his face and brushed his thumb over her lower lip, settling into the soft cleft at its centre. "I can still remember the taste of you. Sweet and fresh like a ripe apricot. I wonder if you taste the same."

Spellbound, all sensible thought fled. "And you," she dipped her head to his neck and inhaled deeply, feeling his sharp intake of breath under her hands that lay upon his chest. "You still smell the same. Like leather and fresh air. I used to dream of that. I'd wake up filled with your scent."

"Even though I never slept beside you?"

She shook her head but he stilled the movement with his hands.

"We did not need to sleep together to know each other, did we?"

She shook her head again, unable to utter a single word as his lips sought hers. Her heart pounded sharply as his lips met hers in a kiss that held both softness and power. It commanded a response from her body that was long forgotten. Too soon, his lips left hers and sought out her jaw, her cheek, her ear before settling on her neck—breathing and tasting her as if she were a delicacy he wished to savour.

She let her head fall back, allowing him easier access to her neck, and closed her eyes as sensation after sensation rippled over her skin and deeper, inside her body. She gasped for air, feeling an urgent need to stop the dizziness that threatened to overtake her.

His fingers drove into her hair, around her head, pulling her mouth once more to his. This time she parted her lips under his and melted against his body. The sense of everything dissolving continued as the tip of his tongue met hers in a sensuous interplay in which all their thoughts, all their feelings and all their needs were concentrated.

His grip on her body tightened and she shifted on his lap, closer to him, her arms slowly drawing up and around his shoulders. They felt so different to her husband's who, despite his acid tongue and free use of his leather belt, was physically slight. Guy's muscles flexed under her touch and filled out to meet her cupped palm.

But that wasn't the only thing that was different. She could feel him rigid beneath her bottom. She stilled for a moment and then shifted slightly, closer to the point that she wanted to feel him against her. She gasped at the feel of him pressing intimately against her. Her body was on fire as she looked down at his face with lips parted, filled with an awareness of how much she wanted him.

She pushed her hands through the rough stubble on his chin and cheeks, and edged over his ears and into his hair. With her hands cupped either side of his face, she drew him to her. The time for preliminaries was over. She knew what she wanted. She moved her mouth to his, hungry now, for all that she'd missed over the years. The kiss was deep; their tongues slid against each other as if the taste of each other created only more need, more hunger that only intimacy could satisfy.

Suddenly she felt his grip around her waist tighten and he stood up, holding her easily in his arms. She tried to bring his head down to hers but he drew away and smiled.

"There's no need to rush any more, Angel. I would take the time to savour you." He glanced upstairs to her private bedchamber. "Besides, the solar will be more private for what I have in mind."

He set her down, continuing his tight hold around her, as if fearful she would disappear if he let her go. Then, with one arm still tight around her, they walked up the worn stone steps to the solar. She felt as if she were in a dream—her body heated with desire but her mind registering the strength of his arm around her, and the chill draft that blew in from the open embrasures, cooling and stimulating at the same time.

He pushed open the door and kissed her. Even as they still kissed he picked her up and her legs slid around his hips as if they were coming home. He walked the few steps to the bed and gently lay her down on the grey fur coverlet, whose scarlet lining matched the scarlet of the cushions.

The dying embers from the fire surged into life and cast a rich light over the tapestries. She looked up into eyes that pulsed as hotly. "You imagine this to be my wedding day that you should carry me into the chamber?"

"Aye. It is as sacred a vow I give to you now, as I would on our wedding day."

His words melted her heart and she reached down and kissed him, a gentle kiss. "You, Sir Guy, are still the decent, loving man you always were. I can hardly believe you've changed so little."

"Oh, I've changed. But not for what I feel for you. *That*, I shall always feel."

She pressed her finger to his lips. "Nay. No more words." And, before he could gainsay her, she'd pressed her lips to his and his mouth took possession of hers with a need and ferocity that robbed her of any further thought.

His hands swept around her body, fanning around her back, and lower, holding her tight against him, as their breathing quickened and the needs of their bodies became paramount. She pulled away, panting. "Guy, please, I need you."

His face was grim with control as he stepped away. He gripped the sides of her loose surcote and she raised her hands, allowing him to sweep it over her head and toss it to one side.

She smiled and they briefly came together in another searing kiss before he pulled away and unpinned the silver brooch that held together the long slit at the neck of her kirtle. He trailed a fingertip around the outline of the low opening, watching her expression all the while. Her skin puckered under his deft touch and she gasped as his finger touched the tip of her breast. She could stand it no longer and wriggled out of her kirtle, pulling down the tight sleeves until his hands took over and drew it up and over her head before casting it aside.

She stood, then, just in her under clothes—the fine linen clinging to her full breasts, its near transparency revealing the rest of her body. She felt herself throb and moisten as his eyes strayed down the length of her body.

His hands grazed her nipples as they moved to her shoulders where he pushed the loose gown down as far as her breasts. Suddenly Angelique panicked and clamped the shift to her breasts, stopping it from falling to the floor.

He frowned. "What is wrong?"

She shook her head, not knowing how to tell him about the changes marriage had wrought to her body. He was still imagining her as a young 16-year-old girl, not a woman who'd been beaten and who'd had children who'd died.

He swept her hair from her face tenderly. "Tell me, Angel, what is it? What would you hide from me? There is nothing I would not know about you. Let your shift fall, Angel."

It was too late to retreat. She closed her eyes and did as he bade her.

CHAPTER FIVE

Guy had waited so long for this moment but, for some reason, he couldn't shift his gaze from her eyes, despite the fact he was acutely aware the riches of her body that gleamed in the firelight. It was her eyes. There was an intensity to them, a fear almost. He shook his head. A fear? Like he'd be somehow disappointed? He reached out and smoothed her hair that was curling wildly around her face. "What is it, Angel? Why do you look at me so?"

She opened her mouth to speak but no sound was uttered. She licked her lips as if they were suddenly parched. "I'm scared."

He frowned and shook his head. "There's nothing to be scared of, sweetheart. I'm here."

She took his head in her hands and kissed him. Then she drew away, back, and back again. "Look at me. *Really* look."

Guy let his gaze fall then. "Beautiful," his voice was hushed, awed. He swept his hands down and around her full breasts. She started as his thumbs rubbed over her nipples. He shook his head. "What are you afraid of? You are more beautiful than I had imagined. And I have a great imagination."

"Look further."

His hands followed his eyes down to her stomach and lower, and stopped suddenly. Scars, ridged and white in the light, crossed her belly. "Sweet Jesus," he looked up at Angel, who looked pale in the dim light. "What happened?"

"My husband, believing I was dying and caring not in the least for me, tried to force my midwife to save the baby by taking it from my belly. He commanded her to cut me, which she had to do, but thank the Lord, my

147

husband refused to watch, and so my midwife did not proceed further. If she had, I would surely have died. As it was, my baby died." She gave a bitter laugh. "A reversal of what my husband wanted. Unfortunately, the midwife was made to pay for her care for me."

A surge of anger swept over him. "He was mad. He must have been to wish you dead." He felt sick just thinking of it.

"No. Just cruel. Just selfish. Just a husband for whom I was nothing but a disposable chattel. Luckily the midwife did not agree."

He brought her close to him, covering her with his body. "My love. For all that you have suffered, I am truly sorry. If the man were not dead already, I would kill him now." She shivered in his arms. She looked so vulnerable. He turned away quickly, pushing his fingers through his hair, twisting one way and then another, as conflicting feelings, of anger, guilt, regret and pity waged inside. He did not know what to do, what to think. All he could feel was his beautiful Angel, vulnerable and sad beside him. He needed to make her comfortable once more. He plucked a robe and turned back to her, pulling it round her shoulders, hiding her beautiful body, as well as the scars.

She pulled away from him, her eyes huge but averted. She sat on the edge of the bed, the robe pulled around her, her hair wild around her face and shoulders. "I knew it." She gazed away from him, toward the fire. "I knew it."

He frowned and sat on the bed. "What did you know?"

She didn't answer.

"Look at me, Angel. Look at me, talk to me."

He knelt on the bed and took her in his arms. She was stiff, refusing to relax, her gaze still fixed on the fire. He pressed a kiss to her head and she turned to him sadly then. "I knew you would not want me, when you saw me as I am. Maimed. Ugly."

He exhaled in relief, half laughing as he fought to hold her more tightly, to bring her around so she was nestled in his arms as he lay back on the bed. "Is that all? 'Tis me who feels at fault; I feel as if I am to blame. That is all. I should have been here, looked after you. I should have never let you go."

She relaxed then. "The past is done. There is no point in feeling guilty, no point in thinking about what might have been." She looked up into his eyes. "All we have is now, my body, as it is. But it's not enough, is it?"

"Angel," he caught her chin and forced her to look at him. "You are correct. It isn't enough, but not in the way you think. You are as beautiful to me now, as you ever were. So... your skin bears scars. So does mine—to my body, to my heart, to my soul. Battle scars, all. There is nothing we can do about these things and they make you no less beautiful in my eyes. You are... you always will be... *more* than enough for me. You are all that I want in this world." He closed his eyes as her hand gently touched his face. It seemed such softness should have no right to be placed against his battle-hardened face. "I want your body, Angel, of course I do and it's beautiful. But 'tis not all I want." He pushed away the veil of her hair. "I want all of you—your mind, your skin, your heart, your scars. All of you."

"Oh, Guy. I cannot allow myself to be vulnerable. I have to leave, I *have* to go away, escape the future the King wishes to impose on me. The scars go deeper than my skin. They've severed my connection with anything resembling a normal life. I doubt I can trust anyone again. I want no more lies, no more deceit."

He sucked in a harsh breath. He needed to tell her the truth. He couldn't continue as planned, now that he knew of her past sufferings. "Angel, there are things I need to tell you."

"What do you need to tell me that will change what we have now? We are both here this night. Let's forget the past, ignore the future and take all that we can today."

He narrowed his eyes and hesitated. Was she right? Certainly his body agreed with her. He wanted her. And then, if he wanted more? Nay, he couldn't tell her. If he told her, all would be lost. She would leave, have no more to do with him. He had to persuade her to take him as he was, first. He'd show her. He had tonight. It *had* to be enough.

He pressed his lips to hers to stem any further argument. It worked. He felt the words escape into a breath that he inhaled. He focused on her lips, willing her to understand the needs of his body and heart through that kiss. But what started off as a tender kiss, deepened as she whimpered and relaxed in his arms. Only then did he take his lips away. "Lay down, Angel."

Despite the deliberate softness of his voice, she frowned briefly. "No, you want more than I can give."

"You're wrong. I only want what you're willing to give. No more, no less."

But the frown lingered. "And the things you need to tell me? They can wait?"

He took a lock of her long hair—a rich tawny red in the light of the flickering flames of the fire and jewel-like upon the rich silk threads of the tapestried pillows that lay jumbled with the scarlet cushions—and trailed it around her breast. "Yes. No more words. Not now."

Her brow relaxed and she exhaled softly, nodding.

Deftly, he untied the cloak and pushed it from her shoulders, admiring her beauty. He stood up and pulled his tunic over his head. "There are many things I need to tell you. But the most important? That, I will *show* you instead."

CHAPTER SIX

She closed her eyes briefly. When she opened them she saw what she'd been wanting to see; what she'd only been seeing in her dreams and mind and imagination; what her body had known but her eyes had never seen. Even if she'd seen him naked years ago, she wouldn't have recognized him now. There was power everywhere: from the hard, rounded muscles that bunched in his arms, more used to wielding a sword than a quill, to the tight ripple of strength across his stomach. He'd always been a man of control and it showed in his body. Never more so now, when her eyes settled on his cock: thick and long like his body. She shifted her hips instinctively and felt a throb of arousal, deep inside.

She looked up into his eyes and any remaining feelings of discomfort over her scars were swept away by how he looked at her. His face was alight with lust. She could see he thought she was beautiful. He didn't need to say anything. He was right, the time for words was past.

"Your skin is beautiful." The rough pad of his forefinger softly traced her jaw, neck and chest before his hand cupped her breast. "And your breasts." Her breath shuddered from her as he put both hands under her full breasts and rubbed his thumb over her nipples. "Your breasts are more beautiful than I ever imagined. And, believe me, I've imagined them many times."

She looked at him alarmed and suddenly doubtful. "My husband used to say they weren't the breasts of a lady, but of a coarse maid."

"And you believed him?"

"No, it's just that I didn't know…"

"Know this, Angel, your breasts are beautiful." He lowered his lips and kissed the top of each one lightly and reverently in turn. Then he played with her nipples, rubbing them with his thumb and fingers until they extended under his touch. She gasped under the flood of strange sensations that swept through her body, stirring it in a way she'd never imagined. She arched her back so that her breasts pushed further into his hands.

A smile flickered through the mask of intense concentration on his face. Then he descended to her breasts and his mouth found the tightened flesh where his thumbs had just been. He flicked it with his tongue—first one nipple and then the other before he dropped his head and suckled her hard. She cried out as the spiralling sensations suddenly merged, gathered and exploded inside her. She trembled as he drew her more tightly into his arms, holding her until the shaking ceased.

He withdrew and swept his hands down her body and around her hips. He settled in front of her and traced a finger lightly around her hips. She lay back, eyes closed, focusing all her attention on his hands that continued their journey of exploration, further still to the most private of places. He traced a finger lightly around her sex and she gasped and opened her eyes to see his mouth curving into a smile, as he played with her.

"Angel, you are so ready for me."

She swallowed and nodded. "I've been ready for a long time."

He grinned. "Then I'd best not tarry any longer."

He dropped down his head and, with his tongue, lathed the bud that was tight with sensation.

He pulled away, too soon, and kissed her again on the lips. The feel of his hard, muscled chest against her soft skin was intoxicating. She felt heady with need and pushed herself against him, rubbing hard to regain the exquisite sensations that shimmered through her body as her nipples rubbed against his chest, and his hips ground against hers, pressing his cock against her sex.

Any lingering doubts evaporated under the feel of him against her, of the heat of his mouth on hers, breathing her in, her breathing him in.

They were nothing like their kisses of old that had been innocent by comparison. His tongue slid against hers, his body pressed against hers and his hands swept around her bottom, pulling her tight against his arousal.

"'Tis you, Angel," he gasped between kisses. "Only you. I've never wanted anyone more. You want power? You have it all." As his lips met hers once more she realized she believed him. There was only one reason she was with Guy and that was because she wanted to be.

He pulled back from her and she strained to keep his mouth pressed against hers. But he would have none of it. He smiled and pressed his finger against her lips, his eyes hooded. "Patience, my Angel. You might have the power but I would explore your body a little first. Re-acquaint myself with it."

He held her gaze but raked his fingernails down her stomach, stopping

151

only to gently caress the scar that ran across her skin, before descending to cup her sex. And lower…

She fell back against the cushions and grey fur coverlet, as her body responded to the subtle, and then not to subtle, stimulations of his fingers. He shifted lower and she pushed her fingers through his thick hair, grasping it more tightly as his fingers moved lower. "You're so wet, my love." He reached up and kissed her.

She moaned as the intensity coiled and built inside her, and opened her mouth to his tongue, shifting her legs open at the same time. The kiss deepened as he thrust his finger slickly around and then penetrated her. She gasped against his mouth and opened her legs still wider and he slipped a second finger inside her. At the same time he pulled his mouth from hers, and turned to watch his fingers at work.

She inhaled sharply and drew one arm under her head so she could see him better, so she could watch him, watching her, as his fingers slid repeatedly in and out of her: a repetition that was no repetition, but an accumulation of tension taking her closer to that blissful oblivion for which she now longed. Each movement of his fingers was the same, but each movement notched her one step higher. Then three fingers; she felt the pressure and sensations increase. She tried to hold back, to wait for the part of him she wanted, so badly, deep inside of her, but she couldn't. And her head fell back and she cried out as the rhythm continued and she pushed herself onto his hand, wanting him to feel the movement of her, the quivering, fluttering sensations within her and the intensity of her, swamp his fingers.

Only when she stilled did she feel him withdraw. It was her turn now.

CHAPTER SEVEN

Her turn. But where to begin? Her experience was limited, as she'd never had a desire to prolong intimacy with her husband.

She kissed him and slid her hands down the sides of his body, until it reached his stomach, ridged with muscle and then... She sucked in a tight breath as her fingers curled around his cock which jerked beneath her hands. It felt like silk under her soft fingertips. She clenched herself inside, as she tried to restrain her need to take him immediately to where her desire was most intense. No, she had to go more slowly. Savour the moment, as he'd said. After all, it would be the only one she'd have.

She moved her fingers until it touched the end, so smooth except for the bead of moisture that pearled at the tip. She rubbed it and brought her finger to her lips. Watching him all the while she sucked it off her finger.

Then with one swift movement he brought his hands under her hips and pressed his cock against her, demanding entry. She brought her legs up and he slipped inside her.

Sex with her husband had been painful. But now, her gasp had nothing to do with pain and all to do with pleasure as he filled her inch by smooth inch with himself. He held himself there for a long moment, each of them feeling the intimacy of the connection, something much more than merely physical. He filled her so completely that she felt impaled by him, except that it was an impaling that brought no pain—only exquisite sensations that coursed through her body, that ran in waves across her skin and that engorged her flesh that wrapped tightly around him.

Slowly he began to ease himself out of her and she almost panicked until he stopped and pushed back into her. He repeated it, pushing harder each time until she rucked the fur coverlet beneath her. His rhythm increased and so too, did the weightless bliss that ebbed and receded inside her, shifting with each movement he made, until the waves took a life of their own and she cried out, a cry that rose to the oak rafters, to the warm, smoky air that lingered high above them. Only then did she feel the tensions in his body heighten, the movements of his hips grow smaller, yet more intense as he filled her with his seed.

They lay for some time, panting, their bodies slick with sweat, her body trembling from the tumult of sensation that had every nerve ending, every fiber of her body, stimulated.

She closed her eyes and submitted to the bone-relaxed floating feeling that overtook her. Slowly through the mists of oblivion she felt the sharp, tender touch of his fingernails slide down her chest, her breast, before resting on her sex.

"Angel." His voice came out of the dark to her, came from another world, calling her back to him. Slowly she blinked and registered the red lick of the dying flames in the fireplace casting over large shadows on the tapestries and the knapped flint walls of the solar. They met and blended and overtook the tapers that still sputtered in the wall sconces. "Angel."

She turned to him and saw him as if for the first time.

"Guy." She felt, rather than heard, her voice. It breathed out towards him and he seemed to catch it as his mouth captured hers. She rolled over to him until their bodies were touching once more. She moved her open palm, her fingers outstretched, taut with expectation and disbelief, across his body. His shoulders tensed under her touch, and his muscles contracted as he reached up and pulled her tight to him. Her hands travelled the length of his body, feeling the tight swell of his bottom before reaching around and down, between his legs.

He was hard already and, with eyes closed, he pressed his forehead to hers as her hand gripped his cock and moved it against her sex, until her body quickened in response.

But it wasn't the same as before. This time her need was, if anything, greater than his. What he'd shown her hadn't lessened her desire but had exposed her to how great it was—for the right man. Her body, legs, hands, moved instinctively over him and she pushed him until he lay on his back. She captured his hands above his head—his arms, shoulders, and hands, so strong and yet so yielding within her own slender ones. Again she felt her power. She dipped her head to his and sought his mouth with hers in a deep kiss, allowing her breasts to hang over his chest, her nipples grazing the rough hair, arousing them both, as she rubbed herself up and down the length of him.

She rose then, drawing her mouth away from him and rested her sex on his for a moment, relishing the slick feel of him against her before she

154

slipped onto him, closing her eyes to relish every inch of sensation he gave her. It was different this time. She felt again her power and sat upright, feeling him as if he were her backbone, keeping her body together, making her whole.

Then she rose up on him, watching him from beneath lowered lids. The sensations shot through her body as she watched the emotions flit over his face, his mouth, his eyes as she moved up and down. His hands reached up and cupped her breasts. She continued to move until she could receive no more and she cried out and fell upon him as her body spasmed around him, caressing his cock.

They rolled to their sides and it felt more intimate than anything else. Here, they were equals; their hands exploring each other's bodies, while he explored hers inside. They kissed, long and languorously before her lips descended to his neck, nipping and licking, until her she felt the coils of desire tighten within her.

With a grunt he rolled her onto her back and drove into her, hard and fast. His eyes, while still holding hers, reflected the exquisite sensations within him as his movements tightened and he pulsed again, deep within her.

They collapsed into each other's arms and lay spent. With his body against hers, his arms around hers, they lay in silence, both lost in their own thoughts, listening to the distant roar of the sea.

She'd lain beside her husband for years in this chamber, awake, while he slept off his drink. Same place, same bed, but oh, so different. For the first time ever, she didn't feel she had to cut herself off and distance herself from the man at her side. She had tied herself to this man.

Guy softly stroked her but still neither spoke. And then the stroking quietly ceased and she felt, rather than heard, him drift off to sleep. The muscles in his arms relaxed, and yet still held her secure within their embrace. Where sleep, dreams and reality met, she didn't know. All became one with the wind that swirled around the castle, the whine and hum of the wind, reminding her of her promise to herself on her husband's death bed. No more ties.

What was she going to do?

CHAPTER EIGHT

She awoke to the piercing calls of the marsh birds. It was a lonely sound out here on the edge of the marshes, so close to the sea. Once monks had lived in the old chapel behind the castle, finding refuge from the world in prayer, and collecting tariffs from passing boats before the channel silted up. Now it was her turn to find refuge—but not in prayer. In the arms of a man whom she realized she'd always loved and would always love. No matter if she never saw him again after today. And she could not.

Her hand rose and fell on his chest. She could hardly see him as only the barest sliver of pale dawn light penetrated the solar's shutters. She dropped her lips to his chest and up to his neck, her mouth coming to rest on his ear with a nip. She felt him awaken and when she pulled away, his hand traced her face and down to her breasts that peaked under his touch. He watched her with the same intensity as she watched his face take form from the darkness.

"Say something, Angel."

She shook her head. She couldn't trust her voice not to reveal the tears that slid down her cheeks. She turned away and lay on her back, awkwardly laying one arm across her eyes.

"What is it?"

He pushed himself up on his elbow and gently pulled her arms away. "This is no time for secrets. What ails you? Did I hurt you?"

She shook her head, trying to suppress the emotions that threatened to break through her voice. She cleared her throat. "I had no idea it was like that."

Concern melted from his face, forming a warmth that she simply wanted to bask under forever. "It's not, not *for* everyone, not *with* everyone."

Just the thought of him with other women made her slip away from his arms and rise.

"I need to get ready. And you need to be away. The causeway will be clear for you to leave now."

"It's early yet. Come back to bed." She closed her eyes at his touch. "Anyway, who said anything about my going?"

"I did. Do you think you can stay here? You've done what you came here to do. You've seen me."

"Angel, come, there is no need for this."

"There is every need. You've got what you came here for—and more."

"What do you mean, and more? You think that last night was just a pleasant way to pass the night?" He reached for her hand. "You underestimate me, Angel."

"No. I would never do that. I know who you are. I know the nature of the blood that runs in your veins. You are from a long line of noble knights."

"Impoverished knights whose lands were stolen from them."

"It doesn't stop you from being who you are. But, for all that, the die is cast. We both have separate paths to follow."

Wearily he swung his legs off the bed, pushed his fingers through his unruly hair and stood up. He appeared completely at ease with no clothes on. In the soft light of dawn, Angel could see the full extent of his injuries that made her own scarring appear like nothing more than a child's scrape. She walked over to him and touched a long scar that ran across his shoulders, feeling it curve around his body; air sucking into her body at the realization of how close he'd come to death.

He pulled her hand away but held it in his own. "The price of war, Angel. A price I no longer wish to pay."

She brushed the back of her fingers gently over the curling hairs on his chest and the abrasions where none grew.

"What will you do?"

His face suddenly fell serious. "We need to talk."

"Now?" Her hand grew bolder, dropping to his stomach.

He caught her hand in his own. "Stop that woman, or neither of us will be going anywhere."

She cast a glance down and saw what he meant. She felt a deep sense of her feminine power as touched his cock. He tensed and shut his eyes as her fingers curled and closed around his aroused shaft.

"You wanted to talk?"

"Not with you doing that." She slipped her hand more tightly around him.

"You have only now. As soon as it's fully light, my maidservant will arrive." She reached up to kiss him.

157

"You are trying to distract me."

"And I believe I'm succeeding."

He growled, a deep rumble that emerged from his mouth onto her breast. She gasped and laughed at the same time and twisted in his arms as if to get away. To her surprise he helped her turn around and she felt his hardness pressed against her back. She wriggled against him and closed her eyes in bliss as his hands came around and took her breasts, rubbing her nipples until they were heavy with need. As if sensing her arousal, he trailed his hand down and, finding her wet, growled, his cock straining against her back.

Suddenly he gripped her around the hips and lifted her onto the bed. But before she could turn he'd raised her hips and his fingers stroked her, just where she wanted to be stroked. She dropped her head and groaned with pleasure. Each flick, each small penetration was taking her nearer the edge. She pressed into his hand but he withdrew. She opened her eyes with surprise but before she could remonstrate she felt his length slip into her slowly from behind, so slowly, that each silky inch intensified and heightened her pleasure until, with his final thrust, deep inside, she cried out his name for the first time.

His fingers continued to play with her as he thrust repeatedly. Each movement making her want to faint with pleasure.

"You are mine, Angel."

He continued thrusting, one hand rubbing the nub of sensory pleasure that heightened the effect of his movements, the other fingers entering her mouth where she sucked his fingers that tasted of them both.

"You cannot turn away from me again."

She moaned in pleasure at what his body was doing to hers, unable to focus on his words.

"I want you."

Her hands groped behind her so that she could feel his legs, the muscles taut, the hairs rough against her skin. His urgency didn't stop and all she was aware of was his thrusting inside her and the spiralling surge of need that intensified with each deep thrust.

"You have me," she managed to gasp.

Only then did he grunt with satisfaction and pulse his seed deep inside her. She cried out as the tension was released and her body massaged his, as if wanting to milk every drop from him.

He brought her back against him and lay down on the bed. She wriggled back into his arms that held her body possessively. "You will be mine then, Angel?"

"Yes. Here now, I am yours. But nothing beyond that."

He lay silent and she could feel the tension of anger spark in his muscles but he didn't let her go.

"You *must* marry me. I need you. The King won't allow you *not* to marry."

"I cannot have a marriage like my first."

"You won't."

"How can you be so sure? No one can. I've seen even the best of marriage twist into ugliness. My own father imprisoned my mother for years."

"You have to trust."

"I cannot."

A light in his eyes was suddenly extinguished and he moved away from her. He pulled on his underclothes and paused as he pushed his fingers through his hair. She would have named the gesture one of confusion if she hadn't known him better.

"What if there is a child?"

She hesitated. He wouldn't like it but she'd considered this as she'd lain in the early hours of the morning.

"I can still pass it off as my husband's. He's been dead not yet six weeks."

She felt his sudden anger fill the small room.

"You. Will. Not!"

She rose and quickly pulled on her shift. "I will do whatever I have to do. Go, now, before you're discovered."

There was a knock at the door and before she could answer, a maidservant entered, saw them both and quickly withdrew.

She fell back on the bed. "Now everyone will know."

"You should have barred the door."

"I had no thought at the time."

"It matters not. You don't want me here, so I must go. But only for now." His expression was bleak and determined. "I will return."

She felt her heart breaking as she watched him dress, every movement he made was a movement away from her. For she knew she would not be here when he returned. She'd be gone within the week. She had to let him go. She had no choice if she wanted to be free. She'd done what he'd wanted, what she'd wanted. She'd lain with him and discovered a pleasure beyond imagining. But her experience of pleasure was that it was always fleeting. It was nothing compared to the permanence of a husband who ruled her, of a husband who could do as he liked with her. How could she go against everything she'd learnt and trust in Guy?

He gathered his cloak and strode across the room, his heavy feet echoing through the solar and finding a corresponding hollowness inside of herself. But he did not look at her, not when he got dressed, not when he walked across the room, and not when he closed the door firmly behind him.

Numbly she swung her legs off the bed and sat with her head in her hands. She'd had her night of pleasure and so had he. And yet it wasn't enough. What had she done?

CHAPTER NINE

Despite the bright sunshine that filtered into the room from the tower embrasures, and the warm bath water, Angelique shivered in the tub. He was gone. She'd told him to go and he'd done as she'd asked. But she felt his absence viscerally and it brought her no happiness, no relief.

Her heart and mind were, simply, numb. Yet her body reacted acutely to every stimulus, as if it had been awakened from a long sleep. The hot water had made her skin rosy and yet the chill draft that blew in from the tower door as her maid entered, stippled her skin with goose bumps. She shivered and rose to step into the dry sheet her maid held out for her.

Angelique had caught the odd inquisitive look from her maid. No doubt they were all talking about the stranger who'd have been seen leaving her chamber, slipping out through the postern gate. Let them talk.

"My Lady, Sir Richard is waiting outside."

She sighed as her maid hesitated by the door. "Tell Sir Richard I will be with him shortly." Her maid nodded and swiftly left the room.

Her body felt deliciously used and relaxed. She rubbed the sheet against her skin and closed her eyes as she imagined Guy's hands upon her. But the physical thrill of her imagination was tempered with regret and sadness. Nothing lasted, she told herself. Why wait until the joy of their union unravelled and turned into the jealous, demanding cravings that she'd experienced with her husband? No. No more waiting. No more giving someone else control over her life.

Clutching the sheet to her body she walked across to the wardrobe, where her maid had laid out her clothes, pausing to look out at the wide-open marsh, drained at that hour of the seawater, exposing the causeway. What she saw there shook her mind out of its inertia. She turned to see her maid re-enter and registered the look of panic in her eyes that were now upturned to hers.

"Sir Richard says you must come immediately. The King's men are approaching."

Angelique swiftly finished dressing in her one of her finest silk gowns—ordered by her husband for one of her many wedding gifts when he'd been anxious to impress her father, anxious for the title and lands she could bestow on him—and walked down the winding stairs to the Great Hall. She paused briefly and took a deep breath. While she felt immense relief that the King had been as good as his word and had sent an emissary to collect the coin with which she'd buy her freedom, she knew that, until the transaction had been completed and until she'd left Norfolk, she would still be vulnerable.

She thrust her confusion over her night with Guy to the back of her mind. She had to focus. There was too much at stake. She smoothed her hands down her dress, lifted the heavy latch and entered the Great Hall.

She glanced around. All appeared as it should be. The trestle tables were set out, the fire was roaring and the maids were busy. All the men-at-arms were outside in the courtyard, except her steward who was waiting for her, concern etched on his face. At least, she thought, their visitors eclipsed any thoughts he had on his mistress's bed sport.

"My lady! The King's men are nearly here."

"Be calm, Sir Richard. 'Tis what we've been waiting for these past months. As soon as the coin has been given to them, we can leave for the North." She walked towards the open doors and looked out at the busy bailey and beyond to the gate where a line of riders were approaching. "But remember to make no mention of our plans. The King mustn't know."

Together they made their way across the frozen ground of the bailey toward the gatehouse. Her breath was made visible by the sharp air, and the bright sunshine summoned streams of cloud from the rain-slicked roofs of the outbuildings that stood within the bailey.

She narrowed her eyes as she tried to make out the design of the approaching pennants. It was one she didn't recognize. "I wonder who he has sent."

Her steward stepped up beside her. "Whoever it is, he does not look like a messenger. The King has sent someone of standing."

A frisson of fear travelled down her body. Stalwart guards were needed to protect such quantity of coin, but not such high-ranking men as the pennant, armour and horses indicated.

"They must have camped on the heath overnight to have arrived so early," Sir Richard continued. "Strange that they should have waited half a day before coming here."

Angelique looked from her steward, letting his words sink in, before turning back to the approaching band of men. The bright sun was low behind them as they moved east to west across the causeway, making it impossible to decipher their features. But... she had a strange feeling, a feeling that only increased as the group of men and horses drew up before her. The man at the front, his eyes fixed on her. It was Sir Guy.

She felt sick to her stomach. She clenched her hands, willing herself not to show weakness as he stopped before her. "Sir Guy. This is a surprise."

He dismounted and passed his horse to his man. "I've no doubt." He approached her and she extended her hand, which he took and kissed. She let her hand drop, but refused to let her gaze waver from his.

"So you are the King's man, here to collect my silver?"

His eyes, too, held distance. They made her heart break. "That is correct."

"Then you are welcome. Come inside to my chamber and we can conclude the business. You will not be stopping, I take it?" Her voice held a challenge only he would be able to understand.

He smiled, but the curve of his lips held no warmth. "That, my lady, will depend. Business first."

She swept into the Great Hall and then into her private chamber behind the Hall, where she conducted her business. She turned to her steward. "Leave us."

"But, my lady—"

"Just for a few moments and then we will dine."

She waited until the door closed before she turned to Guy who was standing with his back to the fire.

"You tricked me."

"That was not my intention." His voice and gaze were haughty. She couldn't believe it was the same man. "I may have failed to tell you a few facts, but there was no trickery involved."

"You said you were here to see me, when in fact you were here to take my money back to the King."

"No lies. I came to see you and I also came for the money."

She frowned and unlocked the chest within which lay the money. "It's all there, ready for the King."

His eyes, a cool grey-brown in the morning light, narrowed but never strayed from hers. He shook his head. "It's not destined for the King."

"What? Sir, you talk in riddles."

"The King has granted *me* this silver. He has proved very grateful for my services over the years. He wishes to repay the few friends he has left."

"My silver is payment for my freedom. I don't care who receives it so long as I am free."

"The King has proved so generous, in fact, that he has granted me, *you*."

A deathly hush hung between them both. Neither moved. Angelique broke the stillness as she brought her hand to her throat and rubbed her chest in a futile effort to stem the panic that was beginning to fill her.

"I have paid for my freedom." Her words emerged like empty husks—tokens, without effect.

"No one is free in this world, Angel."

"*I* would have been if it weren't for you. I despise you Guy. That you should stoop to such depths to trap me. So it is *my* lands the King has promised you. It is *my* body the King has given you. It is *my* silver that will be yours."

She tried to walk away but he grabbed her arm and held her firm.

"Let me go."

"No. Not until you hear me out. I tried to tell you earlier, but you would not listen." She struggled under his touch but he did not lessen his grip. "You were always mine, all along. The King agreed to a match as recompense for my services. You were never going to be free. The King was determined to marry you off, the more so for your determination not to be married. But I wanted *you*, to want *me*."

The fire in his eyes suddenly lessened, but the heat felt more intense, as his grip tightened around her hand.

"I wanted to make you see how good we could be together. But you won't let yourself will you? You are so stubborn, so focused on what *you* want, that you don't see the reality of what is around you. Nine years ago you wanted to give up everything for me. Now? You insist on running from the inevitable because of what I stand for. For the love of God, trust in something other than your own misguided notions."

"Misguided? How dare you stand there and talk to me so? You know nothing about me and what I've suffered, and you never will after tricking me into bed with you. No. There will be no marriage, especially to someone like you." As soon as the words of anger escaped her, she regretted them as she saw their effect on his face.

He stepped away and bowed. "Then there is nothing more to be said."

She reached out to him, unable to stop herself. He flung down her hand and strode towards the door. "Where are you going?" She stepped towards him as if to follow but stopped when he turned back to her, arrested by the despair in his eyes.

"You want me gone. I will go."

She shook her head, not wanting him to go now, despite everything.

"But you and your men must be tired."

He hesitated then. "If you are willing to give my men rest for a few days it would be welcome."

She nodded. "Of course. And you?"

"I will leave. I have business in Norwich and then I'll return for my men and won't trouble you ever again."

"I don't believe you. You wouldn't leave now, not after…"

"Not after what? After you've told me you want nothing more to do with me?"

"I don't believe you'll leave just because of that." Her body trembled, but she continued to meet his anguished gaze, clamping her mouth together in an effort to control her treacherous body that wanted only to follow him. "You've too much too lose."

He glanced at the silver still in the chest but made no move to take it. "You understand nothing, do you? Yes, I could claim all that you have. The King has not only given me you, but your lands and the last payment you were to have made him. I have everything, Angel. But it was *you* that I wanted. But it is *you* that you won't give me." He walked away empty-handed and opened the door, but kept his back to her. "My men will be staying to eat and rest. *I* will not."

"Guy!" The cry came out of her body as if she'd been slammed by a body blow.

He hesitated, his hand still on the door and then turned slowly to her. "Angel?"

So many contradictory thoughts—fear, lust, distrust, back to fear—flooded her brain that, although she opened her mouth to speak, no words were forthcoming. She shook her head.

He turned and slammed closed the heavy oak door, filling the silence left by her unspoken words.

CHAPTER TEN

"Sir Guy has sent word he is returning this morning from Norwich, to join the rest of his men, before departing for France." She ignored her steward's raised brow and rose from her accounts and paced to the window.

She barely registered the sweeping views across the marshes to the upland heath, still white under a veil of frost. Since he'd left, three days earlier, her thoughts had been filled with him—nothing but him.

"Good." She turned and paced back to the table, alternately flexing and fisting her hands as she walked.

"So am I to understand that the voyage north is to be delayed again?" Daily he asked her when they would be sailing for the north, and daily she'd delayed it.

"Yes. We are going nowhere today. Make sure we provide a good dinner for him and proper accommodation. Make sure he is comfortable. Make sure..."

"Yes my lady?"

How could she tell him to make sure he stayed this time?

She waved her hand in dismissal and sat down at her papers. But the neat figures swirled before her eyes and all she saw was his face. She closed her eyes but the intensity of her feelings increased as the reality around her faded, giving way to the memory of being alone with him, of the heat of their connection, and the stony, empty loss she'd felt ever since he'd left her.

She rarely cried since the first beatings she'd received at the hands of her husband. Then, she'd realized that feelings were not going to protect her, they would make her more vulnerable. Now, she blinked and rubbed her eyes free of the unwelcome tears, but still they came and she gave up as her tears splashed onto the pages of accounts, smearing the ink. Nothing mattered—not her money, not her freedom—compared to her love for Guy.

Suddenly she heard the thunder of hooves across the bridge. Heart pounding, she brushed away her tears and descended to the hall and out to the bailey. But instead of Guy, tall and imposing, filling the space with his presence, she was shocked to see the Bishop of Norwich being helped stiffly from his horse.

"My Lord Bishop! I bid you welcome."

"My lady. I trust you are well. And where is Sir Guy?" The bishop looked over her shoulder as if expecting him to appear at any second.

Angelique contained her confusion beneath the mask she'd habitually worn before her husband. In her experience it never served any purpose to show men her thoughts. "Sir Guy is not here at present."

"But he is due back today? I have only today to bless the marriage, as the King has requested."

"I believe Sir Guy will be here today but the marriage—"

"Needs to be performed as soon as possible. I have a boat leaving Blakeney Haven on the tide later today."

Before Angelique could remonstrate further, Sir Guy and his squire came cantering through the gate. He rode into the square of packed earth sending chickens and children flying. He swung off his horse and approached them, his face lowered and serious.

"Apologies for keeping you waiting, my Lord Bishop. But I have only just heard that the King sent you here."

"You are in particular favour, Sir Guy. The King asked me to come personally and bless your union."

"No!" Angelique's voice sounded louder than she'd intended. It would not pay to alienate the bishop. "My Lord Bishop, I simply mean the bans have not yet been posted."

"A recent legality for which the King has given dispensation." He turned to Guy. "No need to worry about the bans, Sir Guy. Let us proceed with the business of marriage and then I can be on my way."

Only then did Sir Guy turn to her, although his words were aimed elsewhere. "Bishop, if you'd excuse Lady Gresham and myself for a few moments."

The bishop grumbled under his breath, but waved his hand in agreement as her steward escorted him into the Great Hall with the promise of refreshment.

Guy approached her, coming too close, his eyes fierce and challenging. She'd never seen him this way. Not when they last met, nor when they were young. This was a different man. This was the powerful man whom the King wished to keep loyal, not the man who'd made love to her. This was the ruthless man who'd appeared on the same day as the Bishop, to complete his plans after all.

"Your solar, my lady?"

"Certes," she jumped, almost forgetting his request for a private audience. She could barely think, barely breathe, as he followed her into the solar.

Once inside, he closed the door and leaned back against it. His eyes, underscored with dark shadows, were fierce. She swallowed. There was something about this imposing stranger that threatened to rob her of her words. "So"—she cleared her throat—"you're here to marry me, after all?"

"What do you think?"

"I think it's common knowledge with your men and within my castle that we've lain together. That I obviously consented; the door was not barred... We are married in their eyes already."

"So reasoned, so cold, by Christ!" He slammed his fist on to the table. "And *that* is the only reason you'd marry me? Because you think I would betray you with the knowledge of our love-making?"

"I..." She couldn't speak. Her feelings took over, drowning the words that she'd formed in her mind.

"Because you cannot trust me?"

"I have trusted before and been let down."

"That was your father. That was your husband. That was *not* me."

"You tricked me, Guy. You bedded me under false pretences."

"Only because I wanted you to want me without duress. Only because I live in a world where things are forced. I did not want to force you. We are not all the same. Am I really so bad that you cannot trust me, Angel?"

She shook her head. "I don't know any more." Tears threatened. "I only have myself."

"Face it. You don't want anyone else." Still she said nothing. With each long moment she saw his face fall into a grim line. "Come, we mustn't waste the Bishop's time any longer."

He stood to one side waiting for her to pass. She hesitated when she was level with him but his eyes were hard as they looked down on her: hard, and his thoughts and feelings well hidden. She'd lost him. She walked down into the Hall, knowing that unless she took control she'd lose something far more precious than she'd ever held—an opportunity for a happiness she hadn't known to exist.

"I'm afraid you've wasted your time, my Lord Bishop." Guy's powerful voice filled the hall.

The Bishop's bushy eyebrows beetled with annoyance as he chewed on a piece of meat. "'Tis not what I've heard." The Bishop looked from Guy to Angelique and then back to Guy. "I've heard you've lain together and that my blessing was a mere formality."

"Then you've heard wrong."

Angelique felt a dagger twist in her heart at his denial.

"The King will not be pleased."

"I will tell him of the change of plan myself."

"And the scutage payment? He was expecting payment in lieu of your fighting services."

This was news to Angelique and she looked fearfully at Guy, knowing he didn't have the sort of money the King sought, knowing that he was sickened with war.

"He will receive my services."

The Bishop's disapproving frown settled upon Angelique. "It seems, my lady, that you will be left in peace once more. I will go directly."

She cleared her throat that had thickened at the thought of Guy risking his life and limb in the constant battles in which the King engaged in France. She'd seen evidence in the scars on his body. She knew that his bravery would always ensure he was first in line. She knew that if he left she might never see him again.

"No. Please, finish your meal. You have ridden far. But excuse me for just one moment, I need to fetch something."

She walked quickly across the hall and entered her private chamber where she unlocked the chest with fumbling fingers. She plucked out one of the bags of silver and locked the chest. She weighed it in her hand. The silver had been meant to buy her freedom. And she would use it as such, still.

Guy's eyes were upon her as she re-entered the Hall. But she turned, instead, to the bishop.

"My Lord Bishop, this is but one bag of silver of many. Take them in payment for the scutage."

The Bishop frowned and took the bag from her outstretched hand. "How much in total?"

When she told him, an avaricious smile broke out on his face, as he no doubt calculated how much he could pocket himself in the transaction. "Yes, I'm sure this will be most acceptable to the King."

"No, my Lord Bishop." Guy's voice was powerful, brimming with anger. "It is not Lady Angelique's scutage to pay."

"Yes, it is." Angelique turned to Guy, while her words were aimed at the Bishop. "A wife's wealth belongs to her husband. We are already married in the eyes of the Lord."

"What is it that you're saying?" the Bishop asked.

"We have slept together more than once. I agreed to the marriage contract and I hope Sir Guy does too. I wish you to bless the marriage."

Within two steps Guy was by her side, his eyes searching her face, his whisper, for her ears only. "Why are you doing this? For me? To save me from war, is that it?"

She shook her head. "No," she whispered back. "I do it for me."

Oblivious to the surprised smile of the Bishop and her steward, Guy briefly caressed her cheek. She closed her eyes at the intensity of feeling his touch aroused, and parted her lips in a soft gasp. Her eyes were still closed when his lips pressed against hers. He pulled away too quickly. "Tell me why."

Her eyes flickered opened and she saw his expression was still guarded. "Why? Because I love you. Because I cannot have you leave me again. Ever."

He raised an eyebrow. "Ever?"

She swallowed and nodded, her whole body tense, hoping he had not had a change of heart. He inhaled sharply, took her hand and kissed it. When he looked up into her eyes she saw that his defences had dropped, that his eyes were warm and melting once more.

"My Lord Bishop," he called out. "It seems there will be a marriage after all."

CHAPTER ELEVEN

"… And wilt thou forsake all others on account of him, keep thee only unto him, so long as ye both shall live?"

It was as if the Bishop's sonorous voice came from a distance. It mingled with the rustle of the reeds in the river below them, with the song of the birds and the clatter of a cart being pulled along the rutted road close by.

She was barely aware of the Bishop's presence, nor of the witnesses they'd brought with them, or of the few curious villagers who gawped over the fence at them. She only had eyes for Guy, whose tawny hair was made more vivid by the bright sunshine that filled the porch of the church. His large hands cradled her own, while his eyes, that were fixed on hers, held a promise of passion to come. For the first time in her life Angelique had a sense of absolute stillness inside her, an absolute certainty about the rightness of their being together.

A buzz of excitement fluttered low in her belly as Guy's smile broadened, adding to the joy that she could scarcely contain, scarcely believe. He squeezed her hand and raised an eyebrow, a laugh not far away in his eyes. "Are you going to answer the Bishop, my love?"

She was jolted back to the present and, blushing, glanced at the expectant Bishop. "I will. Certainly I will."

The Bishop nodded regally and the ceremony continued. Angelique tried her best to stop the tears of happiness from flowing but gave up when they exchanged their vows. Guy's face swam before her as the Bishop blessed them both and proclaimed them husband and wife.

Guy smiled and brought her joint hands to his lips. The kiss was as warm as his eyes and as full of promise. "Come, my Angel, we must follow the Bishop into the church."

She placed her hand flat against his beating heart and stood on the tips of her toes and whispered into his ear, fully aware of the effect of her proximity and warmth breath would have against his skin. "I would that we were alone now."

She was rewarded by a brief closing of his eyes which, when they opened again, were darkened with lust. He slipped one arm around her shoulders and they began to walk into the church. "It will soon be over and then we will be free."

"Free…" She sighed, melting into his arms. "I like the sound of that."

However it wasn't until much later, after they'd returned to the castle, and the Bishop had left to catch his ship for France that Angelique was able to escape out onto the marshes. Only Guy had seen her slip out the postern gate and he'd know where she was going.

The sun lay lazily on the horizon, spinning the last of its light across the wet mud, turning the low bushes to fire. A flock of marsh birds swooped and soared in playful formation before alighting on the glistening banks of the creek. She'd always thought such freedom lay beyond her. It had taken Guy to show that it lay within her.

She'd reached the old chapel by the time she realized she was being followed. She smiled to herself as she slipped inside and looked up at the darkening sky through the ruined roof, before turning to the east, where the evening star already shone, about to herald a full moon. Then, without waiting for him, she entered the small nave and curled up on the stone seat, still warm from the sun that had soaked into the ancient stone.

Guy entered the chapel and she looked up and smiled. He came and sat down beside her and brought his arm around her shoulders and gently pulled her to him. She closed her eyes and revelled in his strength: a strength that touched her all the more for how his love contained it. He was not driven to prove how strong or how powerful he was, he had nothing to prove except his love for her. And he'd proved that fully.

"So this is where you come when you want to escape. Your game is up, my lady, I now know where to find you."

"The game was up the day you returned, my lord. I used to come here because it reminded me of you. And now you have robbed me of that purpose."

She felt his lips upon the top of her head as she relaxed further against his chest.

"What made you change your mind?"

"Something you said; about trust, about who to trust. I remembered when we were children and you lied for me when I stole my mother's brooch from one of my father's mistresses. You took a beating because you refused to tell on me."

"I remember it well."

"I trusted you then. And I trusted you with my life all those years ago when I was promised to another. But then, somewhere in my marriage, I'd ceased to trust. Anybody." She tilted her head so that she could see his face. "But I do now. I trust you with all my heart." She melted into the warmth of his embrace. "Umm, you are so warm."

"Keeping you warm is my only concern." His lips brushed first one cheek and then the other. "And I can think of other ways." His smiling lips sought hers in a brief kiss. "First your lips. We must make sure they're cared for first." He pulled away and looked at her.

"Of course. My lips."

"Of course. But what next I wonder?"

She shrugged playfully. "Um... Let me think. How about..." She pointed to her neck questioningly.

"You are so right. How could I have overlooked your neck?" He pushed her coif away and brushed his fingers down the side of her throat. She closed her eyes as his lips pressed their warmth against her cool skin. Shivers ran down her body. He pulled back all too soon. "And where else, my Angel, requires warming?"

She gave him her widest-eyed gaze and pointed a wavering finger to her chest, where her breasts were already tight with need.

He laughed. "Ah, but you are clothed. In order to warm you with my hands, with my lips, I shall have to expose your body to the night."

"It is not so cold. Sometimes such things are necessary."

He pushed open the front of her surcote and slipped off the brooch that held her kirtle together. She could feel his lips smiling as they found their targets over the top of her fine, linen shift.

He pulled away, too soon, leaving two moist patches on her shift where his mouth had been.

"Perhaps you should lay down on my cloak, my lady, so the fur can warm you beneath and I can shelter you from the night air with my body."

She swallowed. "It's certainly an idea. One worth trying I think."

The white of the fur shone under the silver light of the rising moon as he swept it around and down onto the stone floor. She lay back upon its softness, transfixed by the way the moon had robbed him of colour, yet still his eyes held a depth of kindness and feeling that was only for her.

"Know this, my Lady Angelique, I'll always keep you warm, always keep loving you."

"And I—"

But her words were lost as his lips and body pressed against hers, making her aware of every sensation as if for the first time: the delicate chill of the moonlight on her skin, the exquisite friction of his body against her, and in her, and the pounding of his heart, indistinguishable from her own.

THE END

EPILOGUE

Gresham Castle, Norfolk, England, Christmas 1215

The wind was brisk and cold atop the battlements at Gresham Castle but Angelique didn't care. She gathered her cloak tightly around her and looked out across the gently rolling hills towards where the sea lay. A few days away from the coast and she always began to miss it. From here she could almost imagine she could taste the salty edge to the air.

"Trying to escape my children, Angel?" Rowena walked up beside her, leaned back against the flint wall and smiled at Angelique. "A nice try but I doubt 'twill be effective. Henry will be stomping up the steps as we speak. And no doubt Maudie won't be far behind. Goodness knows where the twins are. At least the baby can't move around yet."

Angelique laughed. "Nay, they're all adorable." She patted her own pregnant stomach. "I just hope my baby turns out so well."

Rowena put her arm around Angelique and gave her a brief hug, in an unusual display of affection. "What happened in the past won't happen again. You have Guy now, someone who adores the ground upon which you walk. Besides I've never seen you so well, so happy. Of course your baby boy will be born hale and hearty. "

"A boy?" Angelique raised a quizzical brow at Rowena. "You still insist you know the sex?"

"Your babe never stops moving so it must be a boy! Besides it lies low in your belly and, in her last missive, Melisende believes this to be how a boy lies within a woman. And she should know, she's delivered enough babies."

"Though none of her own yet. I hope she is blessed soon."

"She says she's too busy to have children. As if she has a choice!"

"Knowing Melisende, she's probably discovered some medicine to control her fertility." They laughed at the ridiculous thought. Then their laughter died away and they both gazed thoughtfully to the south.

"I wish she'd return to England."

"You know she cannot, not with a price on Sir Galien's head. Besides she's enjoying herself, living a life she could never have lived here."

"Aye, so it seems."

A shout and the sound of running feet was immediately followed by the vice-like grip of a determined five-year-old's arms around Angelique's legs.

"Henry! You'll knock Aunt Angelique over. Come here." Rowena prised him from Angelique and lifted him into her arms. He immediately wriggled over her shoulder so she had to hold on to him by his ankles as he dangled down his back. Rowena shook her head and sighed. "He loves to watch the bats in the barns. He seems to believe he's one, too. Come, it's getting chill, let's join Guy and Saher."

Once back in the warmth of the Great Hall, Angelique joined Guy by the roaring fire and accepted a weak goblet of ale—she had had no taste for wine since she had been with child—and turned to watch Rowena ably deposit Henry on to the floor, receive the baby from Saher and pull one of the twins from under the table, before picking up her own goblet of wine.

Then, Rowena turned and saw Angelique watching her. She raised her goblet and Angelique raised hers in turn. "To sisters," she mouthed to Rowena.

"To sisters," Rowena mouthed back, smiling.

THE END

Dear Reader,

I hope you enjoyed reading about the three sisters in The Gresham Chronicles. Reviews are always welcome—they help me, and they help prospective readers to decide if they'd enjoy the book.

As I wrote the last scene of Seducing—Melisende's story—I began to wonder what happened next in the lives of Melisende and Galien, because these are two people definitely destined for a life of adventure and intrigue.

If you'd like to read a longer book about them, or any of the other characters in The Chronicles, I'd love to hear from you at saskiaknight@clear.net.nz. For news on forthcoming books, please check out my website—http://www.saskiaknight.com.

Happy reading!

Saskia

ABOUT THE AUTHOR

Saskia grew up in a part of England the Industrial Revolution forgot.

She lived near the village of Gresham in Norfolk, England where, in the middle of a field, hidden by towering trees, the remains of Gresham Castle lay.

Saskia's imagination was filled with the men and women who had once lived and loved in the castle and the bustling medieval communities which surrounded it.

She couldn't help make up stories about them, breathing life back into the people who had once passed under the stone arches that now lie in ruins, leading only to a tangle of nettles and wildflowers...

You can contact Saskia at saskiaknight@clear.net.nz and find out more about her books at http://www.saskiaknight.com.

Made in the USA
Lexington, KY
22 October 2014